BERGER  R

Andrew Savil ing
crime writer who lives in Glouce

Other titles in this series:

ANDREW SAVILLE

BERGERAC
AND THE
MOVING
FEVER

A NEW ADVENTURE BASED
ON THE BBC TV SERIES

CREATED BY
ROBERT BANKS STEWART

PENGUIN BOOKS

PENGUIN BOOKS
Published by the Penguin Group
27 Wrights Lane, London w8 5TZ, England
Viking Penguin Inc., 40 West 23rd Street, New York, New York 10010, USA
Penguin Books Australia Ltd, Ringwood, Victoria, Australia
Penguin Books Canada Ltd, 2801 John Street, Markham, Ontario, Canada L3R 1B4
Penguin Books (NZ) Ltd, 182–190 Wairau Road, Auckland 10, New Zealand
Penguin Books Ltd, Registered Offices: Harmondsworth, Middlesex, England

Published in Penguin Books 1988

Filmset in 10/12 Linotron Baskerville
by Centracet

Made and printed in Great Britain by
Richard Clay Ltd, Bungay, Suffolk

CHAPTER

I

At the bottom of the flight of steps, the dog ran ahead. He was eager to explore the bay again. As far as the killer was concerned, the dog was a piece of bad luck.

The dog's owner followed more slowly. She was a middle-aged woman with a face that was always tired. She had bought this place several years before, intending to move permanently to Jersey. But somehow the opportunity to do so had slipped away from her. The white cottage, the cliffs and the private bay were no more than a holiday home, like the apartment in New York and the little manor in the Loire valley.

She paused on the last step and leant on the handrail. The red setter swooped towards her, his paws skidding on the shingle and the dry sand. He had found a piece of driftwood, which he presented to his mistress.

The woman flung it down the beach. The dog chased after it but lost interest before he had covered ten yards. He had a short attention-span; and the older he grew, the shorter it got. Sometimes the woman envied him that.

The dog veered away and ran parallel to the high-tide mark. His tail waved above him as if it had a life of its own. Occasionally he stooped to sniff the seaweed or to nose among the rubbish that the sea had washed in. At the end of the little beach he made a U-turn and ran back to her along the line of the cliffs.

Often he was out of her sight because the cliffs were fissured with vertical cracks. As she watched, the dog paused to relieve himself for the sixth time in the last ten minutes. The woman noticed that he chose exactly the same spots as he had done the time before. Surely he could not smell the marks he had left when they were last here, five months earlier? Since then, the granite cliffs must have been raked by the storms of winter and early spring.

The woman sat down on the step and allowed herself the luxury of idleness. It was only an hour after sunrise. She had the world to herself. Even the sea was empty of shipping.

The bay faced north-east so it missed the sun. Nevertheless, it was warm for May. Her mind drifted away into the familiar reverie of what life could be like if she finally sold the business and left London for ever. She had a terrible suspicion that without the business life would seem unendurably empty.

The setter began to whine.

The woman pulled herself up. The dog always whined when he found something that was dead. Death was about the only thing that really upset him. She wondered what it was this time. A seagull? A fish? Once she had found him howling inconsolably over a dead rat.

The setter was standing at the mouth of an inlet. The granite that enclosed it on two sides was unusually regular. When the rock was still malleable, a giant might have created the niche with two blows of an enormous chisel. Inside, the ground was covered with an untidy mound of sand, shingle and rotting seaweed. The inlet smelled, not unpleasantly, of decay.

'What is it, Leo?' she said.

The dog glanced guiltily at her. He was shivering. His tail was tucked between his legs. It puzzled the woman that the dog always appeared to feel personally at fault when he discoverd a dead animal.

'It's all right, boy.'

She patted his head as she stepped past him. He ducked away from her hand as if he was expecting a blow. The

6

woman blinked when she saw the first drop of blood. The red was unbearably vivid against the muted browns, greens and yellows of the shore. Maybe a cat or a rabbit had fallen from the top of the cliff.

The dog whined more loudly. He wanted her to take him away.

'It's all right, Leo,' she said again.

There was another drop of blood, no larger than a penny. Then a third and a fourth. The trail led towards the apex of the little inlet. It was dimmer here because the cliffs cut out much of the light.

Near the top of the triangle, two or three twigs poked out of a pile of stones. They resembled the claws of an animal. The tips of the claws were red.

The woman bent closer. Suddenly she knew that it was not all right. Perhaps it would never be all right again.

She was looking at a human hand.

'You know what your problem is?' Susan Young said. 'You just don't care.'

Bergerac continued to brush his teeth.

'Jim? Are you listening?'

The bathroom door was open. He could see her reflection in the mirror over the basin. She was still in bed, propped up against the pillows. Her hair was tousled with sleep and her face was red with anger.

'You care about your job, I give you that,' she went on. 'Though God knows why. It's not as if they show much sign of valuing your services. But you don't give a damn about *people*. Not really. Not in your heart of hearts.'

Bergerac spat into the basin. He filled a glass with water.

'Oh, I know you go through the motions. Maybe you even think you care. But if I fell under a bus tomorrow, you'd just shrug it off. "Poor old Sue," you'd say to yourself. "It was fun while it lasted." And you'd check your dark suit was back from the cleaners so you could look presentable at the funeral. And then the bloody Bureau would ring up and you'd be off again without a care in the world.'

Bergerac rinsed his mouth and spat.

'Well? Aren't you going to say anything? Come to think of it, that's the trouble, isn't it? How often do we talk – really talk? You treat your emotions like they're covered by the Official Secrets Act.'

'Look, Sue – '

The phone beside the bed began to ring. Bergerac grabbed a towel and wiped his face.

Susan picked up the handset and listened for a few seconds.

'It's for you, Sergeant.' She held out the phone. 'Saved by the bell.'

The silence lasted too long for comfort. They were driving north out of St Helier on the A8. Detective Constable Willy Pettit wriggled in the passenger seat.

'So what do you reckon?' he asked.

Bergerac slowed for a bend. 'Eh?'

'Have you been listening?'

Sometimes Pettit reckoned Bergerac was growing prematurely senile. Either that or deaf.

'The body of an elderly man,' Bergerac said, 'was found just after dawn by a Mrs Awtry at St Vimy's Bay. OK?'

'Sorry. I thought – '

'I know. You thought I hadn't heard. Well, you were wrong. I didn't say anything because there's nothing to say. Not yet.'

Pettit looked away. He had seen Bergerac in these moods before. It was best to leave him alone. Give the sergeant half a chance and he'd bite your head off.

After a quarter of a mile, Bergerac said, 'Mrs Awtry?'

The request for information might have been intended as an olive branch. Pettit decided to treat it as such.

'She owns a chain of boutiques on the mainland. Bought

8

this place a couple of years ago, but doesn't use it often. Nothing known against her. She flew in last night.'

Bergerac grunted.

Pettit loosened his tie. The Triumph Roadster's hood was down, and the car's cockpit was growing warm in the midday sun. After another mile he was having difficulty in keeping his eyes open.

Beyond Le Rondin, they turned right into the network of lanes north of Bouley Bay. The ground sloped down towards the cliffs. Pettit, who was meant to be navigating, pored over the large-scale map on his lap. It took him a moment to work out where they were. By then it was too late.

'Sarge – I'm afraid we've missed it.'

Bergerac swore. The lane was too narrow to turn the car. He reversed for fifty yards.

'It should be that white gate,' Pettit said. He added under his breath: 'I hope.'

To his relief the topmost bar of the gate was labelled SEA VIEW.

Pettit scrambled out of the car to open the gate. 'Imaginative name,' he said, hoping to raise a smile. 'How did they think of it?'

Bergerac said nothing. He was staring out to sea.

Beyond the gate was a short, unmetalled drive. Mrs Awtry's house was unusually modest for a millionaire's: it was a trim, L-shaped cottage, surrounded by an unkempt garden. The front door stood open.

The drive led up to a patch of tarmac in the angle of the L. Bergerac parked between the police car and the ambulance that were already there. As he switched off the engine a dog began to bark.

A red setter cantered round the corner of the house. Still barking, he charged towards the Triumph. As he drew level with the front bumper, he stopped abruptly. He sniffed the nearside wheel, then lifted a rear leg and released a stream of urine against it.

Pettit gave a snort of laughter, which, with belated tact, he changed to a cough.

'I must apologize. Excitement always makes him incontinent.' A young woman was standing in the doorway. 'I presume you gentleman are police officers?'

A sturdy woman police constable appeared behind her.

'Yes, madam,' she said. 'Detective Sergeant Bergerac and Detective Constable Pettit, from the Bureau des Etrangers. This is Mrs Awtry,' she added as an afterthought.

Bergerac got out of the car. The dog leapt up at him, placing his front paws on Bergerac's forearms. To judge by the grey in his muzzle, the dog was long past his prime; and he smelt abominable.

'Down, Leo,' Mrs Awtry said wearily. She moved towards him.

The dog licked Bergerac's face, jumped down and ran back to his mistress. Bergerac brushed ineffectually at the red hairs on his dark blue jacket.

'It's all these strange men,' his owner explained. 'He doesn't quite know what to make of them.'

The sunlight was unkind to Mrs Awtry. It stripped away the illusion of youth: it showed the lines on her face and the grey in her hair. She wore a pair of faded jeans and a sweatshirt.

The WPC coughed. 'The scene-of-the-crime team's down at the beach, Sergeant,' she said. 'You'll have to walk. Can't get a car closer than this. If you follow the path round the side of the house, you come to the steps down to the bay.'

Pettit turned to go, but Bergerac hesitated.

'Your private beach, Mrs Awtry?'

She nodded. 'In a manner of speaking. It sounds better than it is. There's not much sand and it gets very little sun.'

'Do you keep a boat there?'

'No – I like to keep on dry land if I can.'

'Would you mind telling me what the body looked like?'

Mrs Awtry shrugged. 'I didn't see much of it. Leo found it. It wasn't even buried – just covered with shingle and seaweed and bits of driftwood. But a hand was poking out. And . . . the fingertips were missing.'

'What do you mean?'

'Just that, Sergeant. I imagine someone had cut them off.'

Bergerac swallowed. 'What did you do then?'

'Well, I knew I shouldn't disturb the body. But I wasn't completely sure he was dead. Or even if it was a he. I'm not an expert, you see.'

'So you looked for the face?'

'Yes.' Mrs Awtry swayed on her feet. She would have fallen if Bergerac had not caught her arm. 'But it wasn't any use. There wasn't a face.'

The WPC cleared her throat. 'Someone had . . . well, knocked it in. All of a piece with the hand.'

Bergerac glanced at her. 'Teeth?'

'No use. The man wore dentures. They were gone too.'

He turned back to Mrs Awtry. 'It must have been a hell of a shock. You should be lying down.'

Mrs Awtry jerked her head at the WPC. 'I've had the tea and sympathy, thanks. The last thing I want to do is lie down. You know what happens when you sleep, Sergeant. You dream.'

'I'll get the doctor to look in when he's finished on the beach,' Bergerac said.

'If you want.' She hesitated. 'The only other thing I saw wasn't quite so horrific. But it was out of place. And that somehow made it worse.'

'What was that?'

'It was an orchid, lying near the . . . near the head. Still

11

quite fresh. Rather pretty actually: white, with very dark spots – almost black; the petals were like wings.'

'Yes, dear,' the WPC said. 'Now, you come and have a nice sit-down.'

Leo rubbed his head against his mistress's leg.

Mrs Awtry resisted the gentle pull of the WPC's arm. She stared up at Bergerac. 'You know what I think it was?' she said softly. ' A flower for the dead.'

CHAPTER
2

Susan opened the last of her letters and sighed with exasperation.

'I might have known,' she muttered.

Tim Hobson, her partner, looked up. 'Trouble?'

She shrugged. 'No more than usual. Just another five-page diatribe from Mrs Elsted.'

She skimmed through the letter. The reception area of Hobson and Young was full of Saturday morning browsers, but for once none of them was demanding the personal attention of a partner. Hobson crossed the office to the coffee machine. He poured cups for both of them and carried them over to Susan.

She made a face at him. 'Special treatment?'

He perched on the corner of her desk. 'It's not just Mrs Elsted, is it?' he said. 'You've been snarling away at anything that moved since you came through the door.'

Susan sipped her coffee. 'Is it that obvious?'

Hobson nodded. 'Do you want me to handle Mrs Elsted?'

'No – she's my job. And I'll be tactful, I promise. She's too important to risk antagonizing.'

'It's the bungalow again?'

'What else? She doesn't make a murmur about the commercial leases we handle for her. But the bungalow's something else again. What does she say?' Susan leafed through the letter. 'Here it is. "The place has deep personal associations for me, and naturally I wish to be very careful about the tenants." I mean, what can you do? On the one hand she wants us to get her as much money as possible.

And on the other she hedges us around with what she calls "safeguards". She doesn't appreciate how hard it is to let a bungalow like that in May. It's not like the summer season.'

Hobson grinned. 'She's a nasty mixture of greed and sentimentality. Have you got a tenant?'

'At last. A three-month company let – it's a London firm called Apley and Tuke. But don't blame me if they back out when they see what Mrs Elsted has to say about dusting the ornaments and manicuring the lawn.'

'What will you do?'

Susan almost smiled. 'What I always do. Phone Mrs Elsted and make soothing noises at her. Thank God she's at her sister's in Worthing. I feel safer with the Channel between us. It's not as if I can change anything at this stage – it's all signed and sealed. The tenancy started yesterday, in theory at least.'

'No one's moved in yet?'

'Someone's coming in today. They asked me to leave the keys with Roger Rimmer.'

Rimmer was a young but rising solicitor with an office in Don Road.

'It's straightforward enough,' Hobson said. 'You sweet-talk Mrs Elsted, and you pass on her list to Apley and Tuke. In writing. It's up to them what they do about it, if anything. Then we're covered if Mrs Elsted starts raising the roof.'

'Yes, I know,' Susan said dully. 'It's all perfectly simple. I'm making a fuss about nothing. I just don't want to talk to Mrs Elsted. Not today. Not ever.'

'Oh, come on, Sue.' Hobson slid off the desk. 'We both know it's nothing to do with Mrs Elsted.'

Her face crumpled momentarily. 'No. Not really.'

'The usual thing?'

Susan nodded.

'Why don't you take the rest of the day off?' Hobson said gently. 'Sort something out.'

'There's no point. Jim's working. But thanks, Tim.' She glanced up at him. 'So I'm going to work, too.' She reached for the phone. 'Now, what's the STD code for Worthing?'

The support system organized by Alcoholics Anonymous had several hidden advantages; among them was the fact that you acquired some unexpected friends.

Bergerac rang the doorbell of Halton House. The secretary answered it. She recognized him from previous visits and directed him to the garden. Carrying the small polythene bag, Bergerac walked down the sloping lawn. It was very quiet. Below him he could see but not hear the bustle of Gorey Harbour. It was a good place to grow old in.

Wetherby was weeding a flowerbed. He was kneeling on the grass, excavating a tangled mass of yellow nettle roots with a trowel. As Bergerac drew closer, he heard a monotonous humming. It was an invariable sign that Wetherby was happy.

The old man was slightly deaf and in any case the grass muffled Bergerac's footsteps.

Bergerac cleared his throat. 'Robert?'

Wetherby looked up; he was smiling before he saw who it was; that was typical.

'The weeds,' he said cheerfully. 'They're everywhere at this time of year.'

Bergerac helped him to his feet. The old man wore a baggy pair of green corduroy trousers and a frayed khaki shirt, open at the neck. The first thing you noticed about him was the hair: it was fine and very white; and it stood up at all angles from his head in a series of spikes and ridges.

'Isn't that the advantage of a garden?' Bergerac said. 'There's always something to do.'

'Partly.' Wetherby rubbed his back. 'But it's more the excitement of watching things grow.' He glanced up at

Bergerac. 'But I imagine that gardening doesn't seem very exciting to you. Not yet, anyway.'

Bergerac said nothing.

'Have you time for some coffee? They'll be serving elevenses up at the house.'

'Thank you, no.'

'You're worried, Jim.' Wetherby laid a hand on Bergerac's arm. 'Something to do with Susan?'

'Yes. But that's not what I came about.'

'Are you sure?'

'Not this time.' Bergerac was briefly tempted to change his mind. It would be a relief to talk about Susan. And Robert was one of the rare people who knew how to listen. 'In fact, it's something to do with work. Do you recognize this?'

Wetherby took the polythene bag from Bergerac and examined its contents. He held the bag by two corners, tilting it so that he could see better. His face was completely absorbed. His hands trembled slightly.

'It's very beautiful,' he said at last. 'A hybrid, of course – an odontoglossum. You want to know its name?' He peered at Bergerac over the top of his glasses. '"*Odontioda* Mary Thornber*"*, I fancy. I may be wrong, but I don't think so.'

Bergerac fished out his notebook. 'Can you spell that? And, Robert – it is an orchid, isn't it?'

'Of course.' Wetherby was too polite to show his surprise at Bergerac's ignorance. 'But not a wild orchid, more's the pity. No, this one was bred at a nursery on the island. It's a tropical strain, which they developed only a few months ago. Not easy to rear, especially at this time of year. Did you know that odontoglossums require summer temperatures of less than twenty-six degrees Centigrade, but with a relative humidity of seventy per cent?' Wetherby glanced at Bergerac again. 'But you don't want to know that, I'm sure. The polite name for a person like myself is an orchidologist; but there is another word that is perhaps rather more accurate – an orchidomaniac.'

'So it's unique?' Bergerac asked. 'I mean, it could have come only from one place?'

Wetherby nodded vigorously. 'The Orchid Factory, over in St Brelade. It's run by a lady called Mrs Thornber – hence the name of the orchid. I think she owns the place, too. There is a husband, but I don't think he has much to do with the orchids.'

Bergerac jotted down the details. Yet again, Wetherby amazed him. Almost anyone else would have wanted to know the reason behind his question. But Wetherby bided his time, content to hear only what Bergerac chose to tell him.

He closed the notebook with a snap. 'It's a murder case, Robert. Near Bouley Bay. The orchid was by the body.'

'Dear me,' Wetherby said. 'I am so very sorry.'

'I know you are,' Bergerac said gently. 'And I also know you're not even shocked.'

The old man bowed his head.

'The story will be in the *Post* this evening,' Bergerac said. 'But we're keeping quiet about the orchid.'

Wetherby sighed and looked up. 'Are you going to the Orchid Factory now? Via St Helier?'

'Yes – I'll have to look into the Bureau on the way.'

'I wonder if you could give me a lift into town? It would save me having to take the bus.'

'Of course.'

'I'll wash my hands and fetch a jacket.'

They strolled up to the house.

'I hope you will be able to manage Tuesday evening,' Wetherby said. 'But I shall quite understand if you can't.'

'Tuesday?'

'The chess club.'

'Yes, of course. You owe me a victory. All being well, I'll be there. I'll try to let you know if there's a problem.'

17

Bergerac waited in the cool, stone-flagged hall while Wetherby went upstairs. He glanced down at the specimen of 'Odontioda Mary Thornber', which was now looking a long way past its best.

On a table by the stairs there was a collecting box, labelled THE HALTON HOUSE HOME FOR RETIRED CLERGY. He slipped a pound coin into the slot. The information was cheap at the price.

'The police?' The young man's eyes slid away from Bergerac's face. 'What's it about?'

'Just a routine enquiry, Mr . . .?'

'Fisher, Dan Fisher.' The youth had long, ill-coordinated limbs and a fuzzy adolescent beard. 'I don't know if I can help. I'm new, see?'

'Is Mrs Thornber about? She's the boss, isn't she?'

'She's got the day off. But Mrs Le Vare's around. She's the assistant manager.'

Fisher scurried away to find her, leaving Bergerac alone in the shop. The Orchid Factory was a modern, purpose-built complex on the south-facing side of a steep valley between St Aubin and St Brelade. The shop acted as the entrance hall of the display house, which seemed to contain a small tropical rain forest. Several members of the public were wandering through the vegetation with bemused expressions on their faces. Behind the display house were four or five glasshouses, where, according to Wetherby, the orchids were reared.

Bergerac wandered across to the window. The Orchid Factory was set in about two acres of landscaped grounds. The chimneys of a substantial Victorian house were visible on the far side of a belt of evergreens; that, too, was owned by Mrs Thornber. There was money in orchid breeding.

'Sorry to have kept you waiting.'

Bergerac swung round. A slight woman with a tight knot of dark hair was only a few feet away.

'We're having problems with the cymbidiums,' she said. 'The computer's gone haywire again.'

'The computer?'

'It's meant to control the environments in the glass-houses. The different genera have different requirements.' Her voice was calm but firm, as though she were a teacher addressing a class of potentially unruly students. 'It's ironic, really – usually the cymbidiums are the least fussy of them all. Isn't this where you show me your warrant card?'

Bergerac produced his card, which she studied carefully.

'I'm Jackie Le Vare, by the way. Dan said you wanted Mrs Thornber. She won't be back until about six.'

'Then perhaps you can help me.' Bergerac held out the polythene bag. 'Do you recognize this?'

'Of course. It's one of ours. An "*Odontioda* Mary Thornber", to be precise.' She frowned. 'Don't tell me it's a *clue* or something?'

Bergerac smiled. 'You never know your luck. Are you sure it came from here?'

'There's nowhere else you could get it, Sergeant,' she said in a withering voice. 'Why do you want to know?'

'Let's say it's just routine, OK? I'd like to know who bought it.'

She stared at him for a moment and then shrugged. 'Judging by the condition, we probably sold it yesterday. Hang on a moment and I'll check.'

There was a personal computer behind the counter. Mrs Le Vare tapped a few letters into the keyboard. A stream of information rolled down the screen.

'Most people went for slipper orchids and moth orchids,' she said. 'It's the time of year for them. Not many *Odontiodas* – and only two "Mary Thornbers". One of them went to Sir Vernon Prinknash; it was part of a big order – we had to air-freight it to his wife in London and . . . yes, he paid by American Express.'

'Prinknash? The solicitor?'

'That's the one. We get quite a few celebrities here. The other "Mary Thornber" was a cash sale, so we don't have the customer's name.'

'How about a description?'

'I wasn't on duty. Dan might know.'

She summoned Fisher from the display house, where he had been sweeping the gangways. The youth remembered Prinknash without prompting, partly because of the size and complexity of the order. But there was another reason why Prinknash had been memorable. Enthusiasm briefly overlaid the lethargic expression on Fisher's face.

'He had this car – a real beaut. A Bristol Beaufighter, it was. A V-8.'

'Turbocharged convertible?' Bergerac said with sudden interest.

Fisher nodded. '1982, I reckon.'

Jackie Le Vare looked at the ceiling and sighed.

'I'm interested in the other customer that had a "Mary Thornber",' Bergerac said hastily.

'The flower with spots?' Fisher asked.

'The "*Odontioda* Mary Thornber", you mean.' Mrs Le Vare sniffed. 'Dan, you really *must* learn the correct names. The computer logged the sale just after the one to Prinknash.'

'Oh, him? The little bloke with the poncey blazer? He had this cravat. That was why he wanted an orchid with spots. He said it matched, see?'

'The man in question,' Mrs Le Vare translated unnecessarily, 'wore a smart blazer and a white cravat with black spots on it. Does that help, Sergeant?'

'Maybe.' Bergerac turned back to Fisher. 'How old was he? And how tall?'

Fisher shrugged. 'He was old. Sixties, perhaps, could be seventies. He was a lot smaller than me – say five foot six.'

'Car?'

'Didn't notice. We were busy. But I know where he was staying.' Fisher pointed at an ashtray on the counter. 'He lit a fag as he was leaving. And he threw away the matchbook.'

'That should have been emptied this morning,' Mrs Le Vare said. 'Not to mention washed.'

'Sorry – I was busy. You know how it is on Saturdays.' Fisher delved into the ash and cigarette butts. He came up with a purple matchbook, which had gold letters embossed on it. 'There you are,' he said triumphantly. 'What did I tell you? He's at the Hotel de Bretagne.'

Roger Rimmer usually reserved Saturday for golf, for he had long ago realized that there were career advantages to be derived from playing games with men he hoped would become his clients.

Today, however, he was in the Don Road office. While he waited, he caught up on the paperwork which had accumulated over the last week. The bell rang on the outer door, and he glanced at his watch. The old man was on time. He wished that all his clients were so punctual.

The intercom bleeped. He pushed the receive button.

'Mr Wetherby to see you,' Elaine said.

'Show him in, please.'

Rimmer stood up as the door opened. Wetherby pottered – there was no other word – into the room, with the *Daily Telegraph*, folded open at the crossword, under his arm. The corduroy trousers and the patched tweed jacket made him look like an off-duty poacher. He shook hands with Rimmer and allowed himself to be ushered to a chair. Rimmer noticed that his secretary's face was puzzled.

'Elaine,' he said sharply, 'have Apley and Tuke collected the keys for the bungalow?'

'Yes, Mr Rimmer. At about 9.30.'

He smiled at his guest. 'Would you like some coffee? Tea?'

'No, thank you.'

The door closed behind Elaine. Wetherby chuckled.

'What's the joke?' Rimmer said nervously. It was ridiculous but the old man had the power to throw him off balance. You never quite knew where you were with him.

'I was feeling sorry for your secretary. She's obviously consumed with curiosity.'

'I beg your pardon?'

'She's wondering why you're treating me as an honoured client.'

'Well, why not?' Rimmer felt himself blushing.

Wetherby looked placidly at him. 'I imagine it's because you don't normally go out of your way to do favours for retired clergymen living on charity.'

Rimmer shrugged. 'Perhaps not. But your circumstances aren't exactly normal.'

'When can I sign, Roger?'

'In a week or two. The preliminary papers should be through by Tuesday. If you want I could make you an appointment for the afternoon.'

Wetherby consulted his diary. 'That would be fine. I have the Mothers' Union in the morning and a possible evensong at six. Nothing in between.'

'But are you sure you want to go ahead with this? It seems so sweeping.'

'I'm quite sure, thank you.'

'It's perhaps a little impulsive,' Rimmer persisted. 'Why not give yourself a little more time to think?'

'I would only come to the same conclusion,' Wetherby said mildly.

'Or perhaps a percentage now and the rest later?'

Wetherby shook his head.

Rimmer tried to smile. 'Something for your old age? One never knows – '

'I *am* old, Roger. I need nothing.'

'Then what about your family?'

'I've told you before.' For the first time in their acquaintance the old man's voice had a hard edge. 'That need not concern you.'

CHAPTER
3

Willy Pettit paused by Ben Lomas's desk. 'Pity me,' he muttered. 'I'm going crime-busting with Dauntless Jim.'

Lomas said nothing; he was staring over his friend's shoulder.

Pettit turned slowly. 'Oh dear. I think I've put my foot in it again.'

'Come on, Willy,' Bergerac said. He led the way out of the Bureau into the sunshine.

'I didn't realize you were – '

'Of course you didn't.' Bergerac glanced at Pettit and shrugged: just like Pettit, he had mocked his elders when he was a young DC; it was the only thing that rookies did well.

They got into the Triumph, and Bergerac started the engine.

'Where are we going, Sarge?' Pettit had recovered his self-confidence; it was impossible to repress him for very long.

Bergerac pulled out into the stream of traffic on Rouge Bouillon. 'Hotel de Bretagne.'

'In search of Mr Nobody?'

'Whoever bought the orchid had a matchbook from the Bretagne. We're assuming it was the victim, not the killer. If we're in luck, maybe he was staying there. What have you got on him so far?'

'Five foot five, late sixties, grey hair with touches of ginger, balding on top, about nine stone four, about the same build as me – '

'Slow down,' Bergerac said. 'I'm not timing you.'

Pettit spoke with exaggerated slowness. 'He was a smoker. He was wearing a double-breasted blazer, with a hankie in the top pocket and matching cravat. Polka dots – yuk. Grey flannel trousers and recently polished black lace-ups, size seven. Nothing in his pockets besides the hanky. The clothes are British chain-store stuff. To all intents and purposes, they're untraceable. According to the doc, the cause of death was probably strangulation with the afore-said cravat, though he won't commit himself before the PM because he never does. The other wounds were almost certainly inflicted after death, which accounts for the relative absence of blood. The doc doesn't want to be tied down about the time of death, surprise, surprise. But I got the impression that he wouldn't be totally amazed if it turned out that Mr Nobody got the chop around dawn.'

'Have you checked the missing-persons register?'

'Of course.' Pettit sounded offended. 'No one local fits.'

They drove the rest of the way in silence. Small talk between them did not come easily.

The Hotel de Bretagne was a large building set back from the St Aubin's Road. Originally a small nineteenth-century hotel, it had quadrupled in size over the last twenty years. A multi-storey car park and a conference centre were the most recent additions.

As they walked into reception, Pettit nudged Bergerac's arm. 'We've come to the right place.'

He nodded at a notice by the lifts. It announced the Third International Conference on Crime Prevention, which was due to open next week.

Bergerac stopped and stared. 'Of course,' he said. 'Maybe that explains it.'

'What?'

'Nothing.'

'Peggy happened to mention your ex-father-in-law was

25

involved with the conference.' Pettit's voice was suspiciously innocent. 'Maybe he'll send you an invite.'

'Charlie loves conferences. Especially when they let him speak.' Bergerac was well aware that Pettit was needling him. The best policy seemed to be to ignore it. 'We'd better get started.'

At the desk, they struck lucky. Bergerac had been anticipating a long and tedious process: they would probably have to question the manager, waiters, porters and chambermaids; and at the end of it they might well draw a blank, for anyone that had a drink at the Bretagne could have picked up a matchbook.

But the receptionist nodded when he described, as well as he was able, the man they wanted.

'That sounds like Mr Stroat,' she said briskly. She ran her finger down a computer print-out. 'Room 329.'

Pettit leaned on the counter. 'Is he in, love?'

She glanced at the racks of keys. 'No. But wait a minute, I think there was a message. Just a moment.'

The receptionist went into the office behind the counter. Pettit watched her appreciatively. She emerged a few seconds later with a young man with a harassed face and permed hair.

'This is Mr Jollyon, the assistant manager,' she explained.

'It's Sergeant Bergerac, isn't it?' Jollyon said. 'I think we've met before.' He winced slightly, as if he found the memory painful; the Bretagne did not enjoy having criminals arrested on the premises. 'Is there a problem with Mr Stroat?'

'There may be, sir. If we could have a private word?'

Jollyon waved them into the office and shut the door. 'Nothing serious, I hope? I – '

'What name's he registered under? And where does he come from?'

Jollyon leafed through another stack of print-out. 'Julian

T. Stroat, from London, NW3. That's Hampstead, isn't it? Do you want the full address?'

'I will do. Been here long, has he?'

'Since Monday. But yesterday he told us he might spend the night with friends; he wasn't sure, so he asked us to keep his room. His luggage is up there. In any case, he's still booked in for another week.'

'I think we'd better see his room, Mr Jollyon.'

'But why? What's happened?'

Bergerac said gently: 'A body was found on a beach this morning. We think it may be Stroat. We're not sure.'

Jollyon's mouth tightened. 'Does that mean you'll need someone from the hotel to identify him?'

'I'm afraid that wouldn't help. The face has been mutilated.'

There was a moment's silence in the office. A phone rang, but Jollyon ignored it.

'I'd better take you up, I suppose.'

Stroat's room was in one of the new wings. In its own way it was comfortably furnished: the taps in the bathroom were plated to give the impression they were solid gold; there was imitation marble around the bath; the furniture was mainly chipboard with a teak veneer; and the coffee, of course, was instant. Only the television and the kettle were precisely what they seemed. The Hotel de Bretagne, Bergerac thought, specialized in highly priced imitation luxury.

The single bed was made and the room was immaculately tidy.

'The chambermaid's been in this morning,' Jollyon said. 'She would have reported if anything obvious was missing.'

Pettit laughed. 'In case Stroat had done a bunk?'

Jollyon shrugged. 'We have to be careful.'

Bergerac opened the wardrobe and went through the clothes inside. They confirmed the dapper image that the blazer and cravat had suggested. The pinstriped suit was encased in polythene. The shoes gleamed with polish. The trousers were perfectly aligned on their hangers to preserve the creases.

Pettit opened a drawer. 'He was an old poofter if you ask me. Look at these pyjamas.' He held up a pair made of green silk; on the breast pocket of the jacket was the monogram JS.

'Shut up, Willy,' Bergerac said. He was ninety per cent sure that Jollyon was gay; there was no point in wantonly offending the man.

He tried the suitcase on the stand at the foot of the bed. It was new and made of leather. Inside he found a jumble of possessions. Among them was a Pentax with half a dozen unused films, a flash and a telescopic lens. He opened the camera. It was empty. There was also a bird-watcher's manual – an expensive hardback still in its original dust-jacket.

Pettit picked up the book and weighed it in his hand. 'Not exactly the sort of thing you stuff in your back pocket, is it?'

'Maybe he used it for reference at the end of the day,' Bergerac said absently. 'You'd expect him to have a pair of field-glasses.'

'Bit messy,' Pettit said, indicating the rest of the contents. Most of them had slid into an untidy pile on one side of the case. There were dirty shirts, rumpled but clean handker-chiefs, a couple of novels and several brochures.

Bergerac nodded. 'I was thinking that. I wonder if someone got here first.'

Jollyon, who had been staring out of the window, swung round. 'You mean someone might have broken into the room?'

'It happens, doesn't it? Your locks wouldn't keep out a professional.'

'We are most careful about all aspects of security – '

'Alternatively,' Bergerac went on, 'they might have just asked for the key downstairs. We both know it happens.

It's easy in a big hotel with maybe hundreds of guests. You dress smartly, and you go up to the desk when the staff are under pressure. "The key to 329, please." Ten to one no one gives you a second glance.'

Jollyon raised his hands. 'All right. It's possible, I admit. But you have no evidence that it happened here.'

'No. Just a fastidiously tidy man with an untidy suitcase. And a birdwatcher's camera with no film in it.'

'So you feel reasonably certain that Mr Stroat is the man you're looking for?'

'Let's say it's a strong probability.' Bergerac looked sharply at the assistant manager. 'And it's becoming stronger every moment.'

Jollyon flicked a speck of fluff from the sleeve of his jacket with a long, white finger. 'In that case, Sergeant, we'd better go down to the office. When he arrived, Mr Stroat deposited a small package in the hotel safe.'

'The Third International Conference on Crime Prevention?' Barney Crozier said bitterly. 'I've had a memo about that.'

Bergerac grinned. 'Who's representing the Bureau?'

'I am. Which means three days of sitting on my backside, listening to windy politicians and police PR. And at least half the speakers are going to mention Norma Jean Veldman. You can bet your bottom dollar that someone will find a way of blaming us.'

The jailbreak was a sore point for Crozier and for the entire Bureau. Veldman, a London criminal with the nickname of Marilyn, had been arrested in Jersey on a number of charges, ranging from kidnapping to murder. She had been tried and convicted. A fortnight afterwards, she made a dramatic escape by helicopter from the mainland prison where she was held.

'It's not our fault. She was nothing to do with us once she was off the island.'

'You try explaining that to the likes of Charlie Hunger-ford, Jim. On second thoughts, don't. You couldn't suc-ceed. No one could. You know he'll be one of the speakers at the conference? On police accountability, for God's sake. And I'll have to listen.'

'I'm surprised you didn't delegate it, Barney. Send one of your minions instead.'

The Chief Inspector scowled at him. 'Don't come the innocent. You've been talking to Peggy.'

'She did happen to mention – '

'That heads of department have been specifically requested to attend.' Crozier leant forward. 'Of course I may decide that the conference is far too important to keep to myself. And maybe it would look better if two officers represented the Bureau.'

'The Stroat case is going to be very time-consuming,' Bergerac said hastily. 'Tell you what, how about taking Constable Pettit? Broaden his mental horizons. Give him an insight into the major issues underlying routine police work.'

'Got your back up, has he?'

'You could say that.'

Crozier shrugged, 'He'll learn. If there is a tie-up between the conference and Stroat, I might just take him along.'

'It's a big "if".'

'You'd better brief me on what you've got so far. I'll have to refer this one upstairs.' Crozier pulled a shorthand pad towards him and picked up a biro. 'Off you go.'

'The body of an elderly man was found early this morning by a Mrs Awtry in St Vimy's Bay, which is more or less her private beach. The man had been – '

'I got all that from Pettit this morning,' Crozier said. 'Go on from the orchid.'

'An orchid found by the body was traced to the Orchid Factory in St Brelade. An employee described the man who bought it yesterday. The description tallied with the corpse. It may be significant that Sir Vernon Prinknash, the former MP, was another customer that day. The employee directed us to the Hotel de Bretagne, where staff provisionally identified the victim as Julian Stroat of London. There's a possibility that Stroat's room had been searched before we arrived. The assistant manager gave us a package that Stroat had left in the hotel safe. It contained a Filofax looseleaf notebook. The contents suggest strongly that Stroat was a professional blackmailer.'

'I hope we're right about that,' Crozier interrupted. 'We're not going to be very popular with the Yard if it turns out that Stroat was just the secretary of an ornithological club.'

'It's a virtual certainty. The main section of the Filofax contained names, addresses and what you might call intimate personal details. There's also some coded information, which we haven't worked out yet. Might refer to safe-deposits or payment routines.'

'Anyone from Jersey?'

'Not there.'

'It's the first thing they'll want to know upstairs.' Crozier frowned as the implication hit him. '"The main section," you said: you mean there's more?'

Bergerac nodded. 'The other material seems to relate to potential victims. Two entries are particularly interesting, because one of the men lives on Jersey and the other is visiting: Charlie Hungerford and the orchid-buying Sir Vernon Prinknash. Incidentally, Peggy says that Prinknash is actually staying with Charlie. She had dinner there last night.'

Crozier brightened. 'What had Stroat got on Charlie?'

'Nothing very substantial. Just a rumour that he'd greased a few palms in Halifax in '73. Local government graft. A council scrap contract was involved.'

'Any truth in it, do you think?'

31

Bergerac shrugged. 'If there was, Charlie will have covered his tracks well enough. He's not a fool.'

'And Prinknash?'

'Stroat thought he was cheating on his wife. Doesn't seem much of a lever for blackmail, not these days. But there was something else he mentioned. He'd heard that someone had put a contract on Prinknash's life.'

'Prinknash,' Crozier said slowly, 'is billed to speak at the conference. He's one of the star attractions.'

'On the usual theme? How capital punishment and the lash are essential to the maintenance of the Queen's Peace? He's a crank, Barney.'

'Maybe. But people listen to him, and half of them agree with what he says. And he carries a lot of clout. He's got a chestful of decorations from the Korean War; a war hero always goes down well. He's no fool, either: his firm is one of the biggest solicitors' in the City.'

'It's a complication,' Bergerac said. 'If Stroat's right, we'll have to give Prinknash protection while he's here. We're stretched enough as it is.'

'Do you think I don't know that?' Crozier snapped. He waved his hand in what might have been intended as an apologetic gesture. 'To get back to Stroat: I assume the working hypothesis is that the killer was one of the blackmail victims?'

'It's the obvious theory. Peggy's faxing the names and addresses to the Met.'

'Who's handling that end?'

'Superintendent Overstone. Which means in effect we'll be dealing with his DS. You know – Tuffnell.'

'That's one mercy.'

Both Crozier and Bergerac were acquainted with Gordie Tuffnell, the elderly CID sergeant who had worked with them on the Veldman case. He was cantankerous and old-fashioned, but he got results.

Crozier looked at his watch. 'I must be off. You'd better

go and talk to Charlie and his eminent guest. If you're lucky, you might even get a cup of tea . . . You realize we have to consider both of them as suspects?'

Bergerac stood up. 'That contract to kill Prinknash – bit odd, isn't it?'

'Not necessarily.' Crozier swept up his notes on the case. 'A lot of solicitors that handle criminal work have underworld contacts. It's possible that Prinknash has been passing on information to the Met. Or maybe one of his clients felt he didn't get value for money.' He paused by the door. 'You'd better not take anyone with you. Keep it as low-key as possible. Informal: ex-son-in-law pops in for a chat. No notes if you can help it.'

'Just because Hungerford and Prinknash have got more influence than – '

'Stuff it, Jim.' Crozier's face was grim. 'You know I agree with you. Privately. But you'd be a better copper if you were more of a realist.'

CHAPTER
4

The two men watched the Triumph Roadster coming up the drive.

'A remarkably quick response time,' Sir Vernon Prinknash said. 'Most impressive. It can't be more than ten minutes since you phoned them.'

'Aye, they do a good job,' Hungerford said. 'On the whole, that is. Mind you, you have to keep them on their toes.'

Bergerac let the car roll to a halt beside Prinknash's silver-grey Bristol.

'That's Jim Bergerac,' Hungerford continued in a lower voice. 'Used to be my son-in-law, as a matter of fact. He's only a detective sergeant but don't let that fool you. The Bureau tends to use him for things that need delicate handling. If you know what I mean.'

Prinknash said nothing. He was a large man in his late fifties, with considerable physical presence.

Hungerford bustled forward. 'Good of you to come, Jim. I don't think you've met Sir Vernon here – this is Detective Sergeant Bergerac. We're having some tea on the terrace. You'll join us?'

Bergerac nodded. He followed the two men round the corner of the house. The terrace was flooded with late afternoon sunshine. Charlie, he guessed, was attempting to impress his guest with his democratic handling of the lower classes and his good relationship with the local police.

The tea tray was waiting for them. There were cucumber sandwiches and two pots of tea – Indian and China. The latter was intended for Prinknash. Hungerford poured himself a cup as well, leaving Bergerac to help himself to Indian.

Charlie sipped his tea appreciatively. 'Ah,' he said. 'I like a drop of Lapsang. Nothing like it.'

'I think you'll find,' Prinknash said gently, 'that this is Keemun. Of course they're easily confused.'

His face was impassive but, as he spoke, he glanced quickly at Bergerac. For an instant there seemed to be a twinkle in his grey eyes.

'I was saying to Charlie,' Prinknash went on, 'how well your response time here compares with the mainland's.'

'There are two reasons for that, sir. First, the size of the island. And second – in this case – the fact that I was already on my way here.'

'Coming to see me?' Hungerford said. 'Why?'

'I wanted to see you both.' Bergerac turned back to Prinknash. 'But shall we deal with the letter first?'

'If you like. I'll get it.'

Prinknash went into the house by the French windows. For such a big man, he moved very quietly.

'What's this about, Jim?' Hungerford whispered urgently. 'Why were you coming over?'

He broke off as Prinknash returned with a sheet of paper and an envelope, each enclosed in a transparent plastic wallet.

'As you see,' Prinknash said with a smile, 'I know enough of police procedure to avoid touching such letters unnecessarily.'

'You've had them before?' Bergerac asked.

He shrugged. 'To some extent I'm a public figure. When I was an MP I used to get a lot of them. Anyone who says anything controversial is liable to get sackfuls of the stuff. But not quite like this, I admit.'

'Not on Jersey,' Hungerford said, with an indignant wave of his cigar. 'We can't have that sort of thing.'

The envelope was plain and brown. It had been posted on Jersey the night before. The letter itself was written in capitals on white, lined paper that looked as if it had been torn from a cheap exercise book.

Bergerac glanced through it. 'Rather more specific than usual. Don't you agree, sir?'

'You're quite right.' Prinknash leant back in his chair. 'Many of my anonymous correspondents are abusive, and some make threats. But they tend to promise me hellfire and damnation. Alternatively, they tell me, in great and often obscene detail, what they would like to do to me if they had the opportunity. But this one seemed different.'

The letter was only a few words long. It announced that Prinknash would be dead within a week. And it addressed him as 'Snout'.

Bergerac pointed at the word. 'Can you explain that, sir?'

'I have never made any secret of my wholehearted support for the police,' Prinknash said. 'And I've always believed that actions speak louder than words.'

'Hear, hear!' Hungerford said automatically.

'Certain members of the criminal fraternity in London have – how can I put it? – good cause to dislike me. I am sure that none of them is directly involved in this business. But they have the money and the contacts to hire willing helpers. Does that answer your question, Sergeant?'

It was only a partial answer. But Prinknash gently refused to elaborate on it.

Bergerac tried another tack. 'Have you had similar threats recently?'

'There were two telephone calls before I left London, a week and two weeks ago. They said the same thing but gave me respectively a fortnight and three weeks to live. A man's voice, obviously disguised. I reported the calls to the police, naturally.'

'My phone's ex-directory,' Hungerford said. 'Maybe that's why they wrote a letter this time.'

'So they've traced you to Jersey,' Bergerac said. 'But I suppose that was easy enough. You must have been booked in for this conference months ahead.'

'No, in fact I wasn't. I only decided to come last week. There was an unexpected gap in my diary. And it was partly to muddy the waters, as it were.'

'He was invited, of course,' Hungerford said. 'I was delighted when he changed his mind.'

'If the letter came this morning, why did you wait to report it until this afternoon?'

Priknash laughed. 'I was asleep this morning.'

Hungerford grinned. 'We had quite a night last night. A little dinner party, you know. And when the guests were gone, Vernon and me were having a nightcap and we started talking about fishing. Vernon happened to mention he loved night-fishing but hadn't done any for years. So I said, "No time like the present." I mean, that boat of mine's rotting away in the marina – costs me a fortune in maintenance – might as well get some use out of it. And it was a lovely night. Perfect for fishing.'

'What time did you get back?' Bergerac said.

'About an hour after dawn. Didn't catch much, mind you, but who cares? Watching the dawn coming up over – '

'It was marvellous,' Priknash interrupted smoothly. 'But tell me, Sergeant, why were you already on your way here.'

'Has either of you ever heard of a man called Stroat? Julian Stroat?'

Hungerford and Priknash shook their heads. Bergerac quickly outlined what had happened.

'Me?' Hungerford said when he had finished. 'Me in a blackmailer's notebook? Whatever for?'

'Only as a *potential* victim, Charlie.' Bergerac grinned. 'Halifax in '73?'

'Rubbish,' Hungerford said firmly. 'Not a word of truth in it. There never was.'

'And what was my Achilles' Heel?' Prinknash asked.

'Rumours of – ah, extramarital activities, sir. Would there be any truth in that?'

'None of your business, Sergeant.' Prinknash's voice was soft; the expression on his face was still friendly. 'It concerns only myself and my wife – with whom, incidentally, I am on the best of terms.'

'According to the press handout for the conference, the Conservatives may put you forward as a candidate in the next by-election.' Bergerac hesitated. 'That might make it everyone's business.'

'Possibly. But I am not the sort of man who is open to blackmail – assuming, of course, that there are any grounds for it.'

'Stroat had also heard that there was a contract out on your life.'

'There you are, Jim,' Hungerford said. 'Independent corroboration. It proves we've got to take this letter seriously. The point is, what's the Bureau going to do about it?'

Bergerac looked at Prinknash. 'That depends on you, sir. Will you stay on Jersey now? Are you going to go to the conference? Officially, I'd advise against it.'

'I've never made a habit of running away from trouble,' Prinknash said pleasantly. 'I don't propose to start now.' A deprecating smile robbed the words of their arrogance. 'I'm sorry, Sergeant. I realize my obstinacy will make your job much harder.'

'The Bureau will give you protection,' Hungerford said. 'That's what they're there for. Eh, Jim?'

Bergerac nodded unwillingly. 'But you do understand – no protection can be one hundred per cent guaranteed? Not

38

unless we put you in a safe house. You're proposing to carry on as normal?'

Prinknash reached for the teapot. His hands were large, capable and steady. 'I understand perfectly, Sergeant. I'm willing to take the risk.' He glanced at Hungerford. 'Perhaps you'd feel happier if I moved into a hotel. I really shouldn't ask you to share the risk with me.'

'Nonsense, Vernon. What are friends for? You stay here with me. Honoured to have you. I'm an old soldier myself.'

Hungerford's words were rather braver than the tone in which they were spoken.

Bergerac stood up. 'I'll phone the Bureau and get them to send in a team. The sooner we start, the better. Perhaps we should all move inside. There's cover for a sniper in that belt of trees.'

'What?' Hungerford stared intently at the clump of young oaks on the brow of the hill, as though he were seeing it for the first time in his life. 'Good God, yes!'

They all retreated into the house. Bergerac used the phone in the library. He got through to Crozier, only to find that the Bureau had no one immediately available for a protection team; Prinknash would have to manage on his own until late evening.

'That's great,' Bergerac said. 'I can't wait to tell Charlie.'

'Maybe it'll make him a little more generous when the Committee discusses the departmental allocations,' Crozier said acidly. 'You can always bring Prinknash back with you. I'm sure we can find him a nice, safe cell in the basement.'

'Somehow I don't think he'll want that. You haven't met the man, Barney.'

Crozier snorted. 'I can't stand heroes. Get back here as soon as you can.'

As Bergerac had expected, Prinknash declined the offer of a comfortable cell at headquarters. He was sitting on a sofa in the drawing room, tranquilly stroking a cat. Hungerford was pacing up and down in front of the fireplace.

'There's really nothing to worry about,' Prinknash said. 'Not yet. The odds are we're dealing with a professional. He can't have reached the island before yesterday. It's most unlikely he'll make a move before he's made a thorough reconnaissance and arranged his escape route.'

Despite himself, Bergerac admired the man's courage. He was willing to risk his life on his own assessment of the situation.

'It's your decision, sir,' he said formally. 'The offer remains open.'

'Well, I think it's disgraceful,' Hungerford exploded. 'What's this island coming to? You're saying we can't guarantee the safety of someone like Sir Vernon here? Damn it, Jim, it's an honour to have him on Jersey.'

'It's not Jim's fault – may I call you Jim? – it's the system. I've said it before and I shall say it again, loud and clear, at the conference: we starve our police of funds, hedge them around with the most absurd restrictions, but expect them to keep us safe and sound. It's neither reasonable nor fair.'

The voice was quiet, but Prinknash spoke with the fluency and persuasiveness of the politician he was. For a moment Bergerac almost agreed with him.

'We do the same with the prison service,' Prinknash went on. 'You heard about the Veldman escape, Jim? The woman's a convicted murderer and she was held, quite rightly, in a top-security wing. Yet they whisked her away by helicopter in broad daylight.'

'Jim worked on the Veldman case,' Hungerford said. 'In fact he made the arrest.'

'Really? Then I'm sure he'd agree that capital punishment is really the only solution to the problem that psychopathic killers pose to a responsible society. At a stroke, it saves the taxpayer thousands of pounds and averts the risk of the same thing happening again.'

There was a short silence. Prinknash looked enquiringly at Bergerac, as if asking for his views. But Bergerac was not going to be drawn into a discussion about capital punishment. It was already clear that he would find himself in disagreement with Prinknash and Hungerford.

Before the hiatus in the conversation became awkward, Bergerac broke the silence by changing the subject. 'There was one other thing, Sir Vernon. We have a witness who says that Stroat was at the Orchid Factory yesterday afternoon. Did you notice him when you were there?'

'I remember no one who answers your description of the man,' Prinknash said. 'You think he was keeping tabs on me?'

Bergerac shrugged. 'Maybe he wanted to find out who you were sending orchids to.' He glanced at the clock above the fireplace. 'I must be going. You're sure you don't want to come with me?'

'Quite sure.' Prinknash stood up to shake hands. 'And thanks for all you're doing, Jim. It's appreciated.'

Hungerford walked with Bergerac to the car.

'You've got to hand it to him, Jim. He doesn't know the meaning of fear. He was with the Gloucesters in Korea, you know. Picked up a DSO and an MC. A damn good MC, too.'

Bergerac paused, his hand on the door of the car. 'The thing is, Charlie – we're not in Korea now.'

It was nearly five o'clock before Susan got back to the office. Her mood had not improved.

A thirty-minute telephone conversation had dominated the morning; Mrs Elsted discussed the bungalow lease in exhaustive detail and favoured Susan with selected reminiscences of the holidays she had spent there with the late Mr Elsted.

41

Susan had spent most of the afternoon over in St Peter, valuing a house, which the owner, at the last moment, had decided not to sell; he was now quibbling about paying the valuation fee.

She longed to get home and put her feet up. At least they closed at five on Saturdays. Maybe God would provide a miracle, and Jim would get back early. And maybe, if there was another miracle, they'd find some way to avoid resuming the quarrel.

Tim Hobson looked up as she swept into the office. He was already in the process of clearing up his desk and packing his briefcase.

'Your aunt phoned just after you left,' he said.

'Belle? What did she want?'

'She wants you and your nice policeman friend to have lunch with her tomorrow. At the Bretagne.'

Susan was instantly suspicious. 'Did she say who was going to pay?'

'She made a point of mentioning it was to be her treat.'

'That makes a change.'

Hobson raised his eyebrows in a question.

'She's the family black sheep,' Susan explained. 'Every now and then she descends to raid the drinks cupboard and borrow a tenner.'

'I gathered she was *staying* at the Bretagne. Doesn't that imply she's in the money?'

'I wouldn't bank on it.' Susan dumped her bag on the desk. 'I wonder what she's doing here,' she added. 'She's a Guernsey resident but she's usually on her boat at this time of year.'

'You'd better go to lunch and find out. I said you'd ring back. She sent her love to you and Jim.'

'Damn Jim.'

Hobson ignored this. 'She saw him this morning – not to talk to. At the Bretagne.'

'He gets around. Pursuing his enquiries.'

Susan killed the conversation by going to the lavatory. Tim meant well but sometimes his sympathy was tiring. In her more cynical moments she occasionally wondered whether his sympathetic concern about her relationship with Jim was really just a cloak for malicious interest.

When she came back into the office, Tim had left. But the phone on his desk was ringing. She picked it up.

'Could I speak to Mr Hobson, please?' The voice belonged to an old woman; Susan thought she detected an undercurrent of panic.

'I'm afraid he's left the office. Can I help? I'm his partner.'

'It's about the key. He said he'd drop it in this afternoon.' The voice rose to a wail. 'But he hasn't come. And he was going to give us a lift into St Helier.'

Susan reached for a pad. 'The key for where?'

'The key for the flat. My sister and I, we've been waiting for hours.'

The story tumbled out. The two sisters had been staying in a hotel in Rozel. They liked Jersey so much and, as a result, they had decided to extend their holiday by another fortnight. Their hotel was rather expensive so that nice Mr Hobson had fixed them up with a flat off Havre des Pas; and he had promised to pick them up, with the key, this afternoon, and take them to the flat in person.

The kindness was typical of Tim; so, too, was the fact that he had apparently forgotten all about the old ladies.

'He may be on his way to you,' Susan said. 'If you can hold on a moment, I'll just check. The flat's in Marett Road, you say?'

As she had suspected, the keys were still on the rack, and the details of the holiday let were buried in Tim's in-tray. She swore silently and returned to the phone.

'I'm *so* sorry. It looks as if Mr Hobson was unexpectedly called away. But I'll come over and collect you myself.'

A moment later, she put down the phone with a sigh of

exasperation. So much for getting home early. But the job had to come first.

She locked up the office. As she was climbing into the jeep, it occurred to her that she was being inconsistent. Jim Bergerac put his job first. That was precisely what she disliked about him.

The round-trip to Rozel took nearly twice as long as she had expected. This was partly due to an accident that caused a long hold-up on the B38, just north of St Martin's church. Then, at the hotel, she found her two passengers in an advanced state of panic. A handbag had been mislaid and they were sure that the management was trying to overcharge them in the sundries section of their bill.

'Sweet sherry?' wailed the elder of the two sisters. 'But I *never* drink sweet sherry.'

By the time Susan had sorted this out, it was after six o'clock. Because of the accident she had to take a slightly longer route, via the B46, back to St Helier.

As they drove into the village of Maufant, she caught sight of Mrs Elsted's beloved bungalow. It was an unattractive building, dating from the 1940s, up on her left beyond the glasshouses on the outskirts of the village. A large grey car with rakish lines was tucked into the little drive at the side. Apley and Tuke's representative was obviously in residence.

Susan dropped the sisters at their flat in Marett Road. They tried her patience sorely by requiring intensive training in how to operate the front-door lock, the cooker and the central heating. But when she finally left, the warmth of their gratitude shamed her.

She got home a little before 7.30. Bergerac's car was not outside. The house was in darkness. Inside it seemed cold and unlived-in. Her possessions looked shabby and subtly alien, as if they really belonged to someone else.

Susan bit her lip and played back the tape on the answering-machine.

44

No Jim. No messages.

It was time to take herself in hand, before tiredness and depression overwhelmed her. She ran a bath and emptied half a bottle of foam into it. On the shelf behind the taps she lined up a bottle of sparkling wine, a glass and one of the paperback crime novels that Bergerac despised her for reading.

Something was missing. You couldn't have a party, even for one person, without music.

She fetched the radio-cassette player. She switched on the radio and turned it to a rock station. They were playing a raunchy little number that was at least twenty years old.

Susan poured herself a glass of wine, swallowed half of it, and did a slow striptease to the beat of the music. Somewhere on the other side of the steam there might be an audience of millions. You should always do your best, because someone might be watching. She stepped into the bath and reached for her glass.

At that moment the bathroom door opened.

'Hello, love,' Bergerac said. He peered through the steam. 'Is this a party for one, or can anyone join in?'

CHAPTER
5

The present management had recently lavished a great deal of money on the Marine Bar of the Hotel de Bretagne. Susan Young had not been here since the programme of alterations had been completed. On the whole she was inclined to feel that she hadn't missed much.

She walked towards the bar, where her aunt was perched insecurely on a stool. Some things hadn't changed. The room was part of the Victorian core of the building. It had originally been designed as a ballroom. As you came into it, your eyes were still drawn towards the great south windows that overlooked the sea and Elizabeth Castle.

The current management had introduced many innovations. It liked patterns and it liked the colour turquoise. It also had a fondness for cast-iron furniture of the kind designed to stand unmoved in gardens that are regularly swept by hurricanes. It had installed wall-lights, which gave out very little light but added an unexpectedly Tudor-bethan motif. The walls were further adorned by a large but undistinguished collection of marine oil-paintings, a job lot that the managing director's first wife was reputed to have bought by accident at Sotheby's.

'Where's Jim?' Belle Young asked her niece. 'Mislaid him again?' She pointed accusingly with her cigarette at a passing waiter, and her voice rose to a gale-force bellow. 'A large pink gin and a large gin and tonic. We'll be outside.'

'He's in reception. He wanted a word with the manager.'

Susan followed her aunt on to the terrace beyond the south windows. The big room behind them was already crowded. The Marine Bar's décor might not be to everyone's taste, but the Bretagne's Sunday lunches were excellent. They found an empty table by the parapet.

'What are you doing here, Belle?' Susan said as she sat down.

'No need to sound *quite* so surprised, dear. I have to stay somewhere while Malton's refit the *Bluebell*.'

'But it's not exactly cheap. Nor's Malton's, for that matter. It's the sort of yard that caters for the likes of Charlie Hungerford.'

Belle lit another cigarette from the stub of the old. 'It's quite beyond me why you should imagine me to be penniless. I'm doing very well, thank you.'

'Come off it. You're just a water gypsy.'

Belle chuckled. 'All right. You remember Cousin Cecil died at the end of last year?'

Susan nodded.

'Well, he left me a little legacy.' Belle sniffed. 'It was the least he could do after spending half his life trying to pretend I didn't exist.'

'So you're rich?'

'Not for long, dear. You know how it is with me. Easy come, easy go.'

The waiter arrived with their drinks. Belle consulted Susan and ordered an orange juice for Bergerac.

'What's keeping him?' she asked.

'Work. One of the guests here got himself murdered.'

'That Stroat man? I saw it in the paper. Creepy.'

Susan glanced into the bar and saw Bergerac enter by the far door. 'Oh, there he is.'

She waved, but he appeared not to see her. She watched him cross the room to the small triangular stage that projected from the wall opposite the long counter of the bar. A woman in a low-cut black dress was sitting behind the grand piano. She was apparently recharging herself with alcohol between numbers.

Susan felt the familiar misery welling up inside her. Last night was last night. It was firmly in the past. It had changed nothing: Jim was still a bastard. He must realize how much she needed him. Not when he had a moment to spare. Now.

'You've nothing to worry about with her,' Belle said roughly. She was staring in the same direction as Susan. 'Mutton dressed as lamb, my dear. Pound to a penny he's working. *That's* what you need to worry about.'

Susan shook her head slowly. 'I don't know any more. I just don't know.'

'Bergerac. Jersey State Police.'

'Well, that's an unusual line of approach,' the piano-player said. She leant forward, so her breasts were resting on the top of the piano. 'Have much success with it?'

Bergerac sighed. 'Mr Jollyon suggested I had a word with you.'

'Why?' Her eyelashes fluttered. They were false but her alarm was genuine. 'What does he say I've done?'

'Nothing. You're Anne-Marie, aren't you?'

'That's the name I work under, yes.'

'I can get your real name from Mr Jollyon, if I need to.' Bergerac hesitated, trying to assess whether her fear was merely an automatic response to meeting a policeman. 'He said you might be able to tell me something about Julian Stroat.'

The alarm was still there. Anne-Marie toyed with her glass. Generations of other glasses had left their traces on the piano. Yesterday's *Post* lay beside a pile of sheet music. On the front page there was a photograph of Prinknash. EX-MP TO SPEAK AT CONFERENCE. But the main headline was BODY ON THE BEACH.

'The bloke who got done in?' Anne-Marie said. 'How can *I* help? I just play the piano round here.'

Bergerac glanced down at her hands. They were square,

competent and slightly grubby. The nail varnish was chipped in several places.

'And sometimes you play requests for customers. Two of the barmen have separately said you played requests for Stroat. One of them said you joked about it, because he paid you a fiver a time.'

'Well, why not?' she said, with a sudden spurt of anger. 'I have to get what I can. Do you know what this job pays? It's peanuts! Bloody slave labour. If it weren't for the tips, I could earn more packing tomatoes. The hourly rate's a damn sight better.'

'It's no crime to talk to Stroat. What sort of things did he want?'

'Ballads, mainly. "My Way", "Over the Rainbow", that sort of stuff. Nothing very lively.'

'Did he ever talk to you, besides to ask for songs?' Bergerac persisted. 'About what he was doing on the island, for instance? About his friends? Was he ever with anyone else?'

She shook her head. 'He didn't want to talk to *me*. He wasn't that type. Wasn't interested. As far as he was concerned, I was just a human jukebox. Put the money in, and out the music comes. Most men aren't like that, thank God. Get them away from their wives, and they're interested enough, all right.'

Bergerac wondered how a man of any age could find her attractive. Something of what he was thinking must have shown in his eyes.

'You don't believe me?' Her face flared with anger again. 'See that bloke there?' She tapped the photograph in front of her. 'He's famous, right? He was in here Friday lunchtime, and I could feel his eyes on me. Then he came over. Know what he asked me to play? "Ain't Misbehavin'". I know what *he* wanted.'

'Prinknash? Was he with someone, by any chance? Stroat?'

49

Anne-Marie appeared not to have heard the question. 'But he was a mean bugger. I mean, it's understood, isn't it? If I do a song for you, you give me a little token of thanks.'

Bergerac took out his wallet and removed a five-pound note. He held it between his fingers.

'A fiver would be generous,' he said.

Her hand moved towards the note; his moved away.

'He wasn't with Stroat,' Anne-Marie said. 'I don't think Stroat was there on Friday.'

'So who was he with?' Bergerac allowed her to take the note from his fingers.

She stuffed it between her breasts, just like the whores and barmaids did in old films. 'Jack Thornber. Now he's another mean bugger. He practically lives here but I've never seen him buy anyone a drink. Least of all me, though he likes an eyeful, like the rest of them.'

'Thornber? Any relation to the woman who runs the Orchid Factory?'

'Husband. But she wears the trousers, believe you me.'

Bergerac stared out into the bar. 'Is he here today?'

Anne-Marie laughed harshly. 'Not today, and not for several days to come. Jacko went down with scarlet fever yesterday.'

'You're kidding. People don't get that nowadays.'

'Well, Jacko has, Mr Clever. You live and learn, don't you?'

Bergerac turned to go. On the edge of the stage he paused.

'Do me a favour, will you? Play "Bridge over Troubled Waters".'

'What's it worth to you?'

He grinned. 'You should own this hotel by now. You drive a hard bargain.' He gave her a pound.

For the first time, her face lightened, and she smiled at him. She was unexpectedly transformed. The anger, the fear and the calculation had been smoothed away. At one time, Bergerac realized, she had been extremely pretty.

'Go on, Superintendent,' she said huskily. 'I bet you say that to all the girls.'

He walked away. Behind him, he heard the intro begin. Belle waved to him from the terrace and pointed at the drink that was waiting for him. Another bloody orange juice. The trouble with not drinking alcohol was that there was nothing that was a satisfactory substitute.

Judging by the glasses on the table, they were well into their second round. Susan did not look at him as he sat down.

'You hate this song,' she said.

'I know.' Bergerac smiled at her; she refused to meet his eyes. 'But you like it.'

Belle sighed gustily. 'Are you two going to have a lovers' quarrel? Do you think we could order lunch first? I'm starving. Sue and I have already made up our minds.'

Bergerac picked up the menu. The troubled waters seemed to have swept the bridge away.

'Belle's coming to dinner tomorrow,' Susan said. 'You will be there, won't you?'

'Great,' Bergerac said. He tried to look enthusiastic; he found Belle was just about tolerable in small quantities; but he knew from past experience that it was fatally easy to overdose. He wondered if Susan had asked her just to spite him.

The lunch that followed was not a success. The dining room, which was in one of the modern wings, was full; and the service was slow. Belle talked incessantly, pouring out a flood of nautical reminiscences and putting away an astonishing quantity of claret. Susan picked at her food and avoided talking to Bergerac. Bergerac himself said little: he made monosyllabic prompting noises to Aunt Belle and allowed his mind to drift away.

The more he discovered, the more unmanageable the

case became. Stroat wanted to blackmail Prinknash; Prinknash had an unbreakable alibi for the time of Stroat's death; someone wanted to kill Prinknash, and Stroat knew that; Stroat followed Prinknash to the Orchid Factory, which was run by Mary Thornber; Jack Thornber knew Prinknash.

A web of connections underpinned the whole affair. But there was no discernible pattern to the web: it was a tangle of possibly coincidental links.

A long delay followed the main course. Bergerac muttered an excuse and left the table.

Jollyon himself was at reception. Bergerac asked to use a phone. He rang the Bureau. He had hoped that Wilson or Goddard would be the duty officer; but DC Lomas took the call. Lomas was the same age as Pettit and very much under the latter's influence.

'Have Forensic reported back?'

Lomas took a long time to find out. At last he returned to the phone.

'They got nothing out of the letter or the envelope. No contact traces that couldn't have been due to post office handling. Looks like the sender wore rubber gloves.'

'What about Stroat?'

'You want the report on that, too?'

'Of course I do.'

There was another long delay. Then Lomas read out long sections of the report on Stroat. It was more wasted time. You could sum up Forensic's findings in one word: nothing.

'Oh, and Sarge?' Lomas said, just as Bergerac was about to put the phone down. 'I nearly forgot. There was a call for you this morning. Mr Hungerford was trying to get hold of you.'

Bergerac ignored his conscience, which was reminding him about Susan and Belle in the dining room, and dialled

Hungerford's number. Charlie picked up the phone on the second ring.

'And about time, too,' Hungerford said. 'You playing hard to get or something? We've had an anonymous phone call. What the hell's the Bureau doing? Isn't it about time we had some progress on this case? And while you're here, I want a word about that protection team. Is there any way you can stop them trampling all over my rosebeds in their Size Tens?'

'They're only doing their job, Charlie,' Bergerac said as calmly as he could. 'Who took the call?'

'I did. It was about 11.30. Someone asked for Vernon, and I said he was out. Then they put the phone down. Just like that. The thing is, Jim, I'm almost sure it was a woman. Now if you ask me – '

'Is Prinknash there? I'd better have a word with him.'

Hungerford reluctantly yielded the phone to his guest. In contrast to his host, Prinknash was a model of courteous concision. He had been to church this morning, along with his minders. No, he hadn't any idea who the caller might have been.

'Well, we'll look into it,' Bergerac said. 'But it's an automatic exchange. There's not much we can do except make a note of the call.'

'I appreciate that, Jim. But we thought you'd better know.'

'There was one other thing, sir. You didn't mention that you knew Jack Thornber.'

Prinknash chuckled. 'I didn't realize you wanted me to list my entire casual acquaintance. I've only met him once. Someone pointed him out to me at the Bretagne on Friday. I knew his wife ran the Orchid Factory, so I went over and had a chat. I wanted to find out if it was worth a visit.'

'Who pointed him out to you?'

'A woman who plays the piano there. I think her name's Anne-Marie.'

CHAPTER
6

On Monday morning, Mrs Elsted telephoned from Worthing.

'It's my niece,' she began.'You must remember, Susan – my sister's daughter, Eleanor, the one who married a Brazilian. Luis has got a very good job with an insurance company out there. In Rio, I think. Or is it Sao Paulo, now? They move him around, which is very trying for Eleanor. Housing's not a worry, because the company sees to that, but it's such a wrench for the children, having to change schools and make new friends. It's not so bad for the elder child – she's the sort of girl who can take things in her stride. But the twins are more of a problem. They're so sensitive, you see. They take after their mother's side of the family. Where was I? Oh, yes. Eleanor's coming home this summer for ten weeks, with the children. My sister's delighted, of course. Luis can only get away for a month, unfortunately. He'll be joining them in August.'

'How nice for you all,' Susan said in a voice that was dangerously calm. 'I'm sure you're all looking forward to it. Were you phoning about the bungalow? I drove past it on Saturday, and I noticed – '

'Yes, the bungalow,' Mrs Elsted interrupted. 'They won't mind if you shorten the lease, will they?'

In the ensuing pause, Susan stabbed her desk with a pencil. The tip broke.

'Susan? Are you still there?'

'Yes, Mrs Elsted. Look, we have signed for a three-month lease. It could be very awkward to change it.'

'Oh, but you must.' Mrs Elsted's voice became plaintive. 'I've promised Eleanor that she and the children can have it in July. After all, it *is* a sort of family home. And Jersey's just the place for children.'

One of the other phones rang. Tim Hobson picked it up.

'I'm afraid she's on the other line,' Susan heard him say. 'It's Jim, isn't it? Can I take a message or ask her to call back.'

'. . . So what do you think?' Mrs Elsted said.

'Sorry,' Susan said. 'I missed that.'

'I was just asking if you could approach Apley and Tuke and rearrange the lease so it runs for two months. It shouldn't be a problem, should it? You can easily find somewhere else for them. Perhaps not so nice, but I'm sure they wouldn't mind. And we'd only lose a month's rental.'

Susan tried to explain that there was no reason why Apley and Tuke should feel obliged to cooperate with Eleanor's plans. She also mentioned that rented properties on Jersey were at a premium in July; and that it might not be easy to find substitute accommodation for Apley and Tuke. Even if they agreed to shorten the lease, it was likely that they would demand some sort of financial recompense for the inconvenience.

'Yes, dear,' Mrs Elsted said vaguely. 'But I'm sure you'll manage something. You always do. I must go now – we're going shopping in Brighton. You'll give me a ring tomorrow, won't you?'

Susan slammed the phone down.

'Your favourite client?' Hobson said.

She nodded. 'Don't ask me about it. One day I'll kill that woman, I swear it. Was . . . was that Jim?'

'He left a message – he was about to go out. Apparently "Henri Dupont" is on Jersey, and Jim's asked him to dinner tonight.'

'Oh God.'

'Who's Henri Dupont?'

'He's a French policeman – rather a nice one, actually. Jim's worked with him a few times. The point is, Aunt Belle's coming to dinner, and she bores Jim rigid after about five minutes. I bet this is Jim's revenge. You see what'll happen? Jim and Henri will talk shop to one another all evening, and Belle will get offended because they aren't listening to her. It's a recipe for a totally disastrous evening.'

Some recipes have unexpected results.

Bergerac carried a pile of dirty plates into the kitchen. Susan was already washing the wine glasses.

'What are they talking about now?' she said.

'They're conducting a critical survey of seafood restaurants in St Malo.' He dumped the plates beside the sink and picked up a tea towel. 'They know all the proprietors by their first names, and most of the chefs and waiters as well.'

'Will they be all right by themselves?'

'They're fine.' Bergerac slipped an arm round her and gave her a quick hug. 'They're halfway down the bottle of Armagnac and talking in a mixture of French and English. Henri's oozing Gallic gallantry, and Belle's acting as though she was about sixteen.'

She rested her head against his shoulder. 'I thought this was going to be an awful evening.'

'I wasn't too happy about it myself.' He dropped a kiss on her hair. As he had come straight from the Bureau with Henri, this was the first time during the evening that he had been alone with Susan. 'I'm sorry about asking Henri at such short notice – I couldn't get out of it. He phoned out of the blue this morning. He's filling in for someone at the conference. I owe him a lot of favours.'

'It's funny.'

'What is?'

'Body chemistry, or whatever it is. To listen to them,

you'd think they'd known each other for years. I'm glad it's working out.'

Bergerac tilted her head. 'You're not just talking about Belle and Henri, are you?'

'No.' She grinned and wriggled away from him. 'Come on. You're meant to be drying up and making the coffee.'

When they returned to the living room, they found that Belle and Henri had moved from the table to the sofa. The level in the bottle of Armagnac had sunk by a couple of inches since Bergerac had last seen it.

'Water gypsies,' Belle was saying earnestly, 'that's what we are. It's like a sub-culture, a blend of French and English. All we really have in common is that we potter around in boats in the same part of the Channel. It's a very small world. Everyone knows everyone.'

'It's a very enclosed world, too,' Henri said. 'What's the word in English? *Dévoué aux intérêts de sa coterie.*'

'Clannish?' Bergerac suggested, as he put down the tray on the coffee table. 'They're certainly suspicious of strangers. And they don't like people in uniform, for obvious reasons.'

Belle squinted through a cloud of cigarette smoke. 'Whatever can you mean?'

Bergerac grinnned down at her. 'It's a case of Rémy Martin here, and a few cartons of Silk Cut there. You don't pay too much attention to the rules and regulations.'

'Nonsense,' Belle said. 'Most of us are extremely law-abiding.' She articulated her words with the careful precision of one who knows that they may at any moment conspire to trip up her tongue. 'Most of the time, that is. Nobody's perfick. *Perfect.*'

'It's not the majority that concern us,' Henri said. 'I would never admit this in public, but a little bending of the law does no one any harm. But there is a problem with the minority. From the outside, they are indistinguishable from the rest of you. But they are not interested in brandy and cigarettes. They only pretend to "potter", as you call it.'

Belle shrugged. 'We've got a few bad apples. So's everyone.'

Bergerac handed Henri his coffee. 'You got something particular in mind?'

'We picked up a load of industrial diamonds in Carteret the other day. A fortnight earlier we nearly got our hands on a consignment of hashish. And there have been other cases.'

'You think Carteret's being used as a depot on a smuggling route?'

'I knew they'd start talking shop,' Susan muttered to Belle. 'I suppose we're supposed to chat about hemlines, or something appropriate to little women.'

But Belle wasn't listening to her. 'A route from Carteret? To England, you mean?'

'Or the Channel Islands. *Les Iles Anglo-Normandes* are well-placed as a distribution centre.'

Bergerac glanced at Dupont. Old Henri was up to something. He sprawled on the sofa like a battered teddy bear; he looked as relaxed as it was possible for a middle-aged copper to be. Yet there was little doubt, in Bergerac's mind at least, that the Frenchman's seemingly aimless flow of gossip and flattery had been designed to channel Belle towards this subject.

She had clearly come to a similar conclusion. Her face hardened with suspicion. 'You're asking me to rat on my friends,' she said flatly. 'It stinks.'

'*Ah, mais non!*' Henri's dismay was almost comical in its intensity. 'Quite the reverse, my dear Belle. You see, enquiries will have to be made. I cannot prevent that. And I do not think you would wish me to, even if I could. But I have no desire to trouble the innocent.' He leant forward to refill her glass. 'Or even the nearly innocent. If I knew where to start – just a few likely names – the affair could be dispatched with the maximum of speed and minimum of inconvenience.'

Belle gnawed her lower lip. Bergerac watched her out of the corner of his eye. She was a plump, untidy woman, who had little time for most of the traditional virtues. He guessed that she had constructed her own code of standards. Disloyalty to her friends would be taboo; but so, on the other hand, would be professional crime.

At last she gave a sigh. 'I don't like this, Henri. But I can see you've got a job to do.' Her hands tightened round the fragile balloon glass. 'If you've got to interrogate anyone, you might as well begin with these.'

She reeled off half a dozen names. Four were based on Guernsey; one in Carteret; and the last of them was Jack Thornber.

'Thornber?' Bergerac spilled his coffee. 'You know him?'

'Not well.' Belle sniffed. 'No one knows him well. He's got a personality that would sour milk at fifty paces.'

Dupont raised his eyebrows. 'You've come across him in another context, Jim?'

'Let's say he's on the periphery of a case I'm working on.'

'"The Body on the Beach"?' Susan said. 'Do you think . . .?'

Henri chuckled. 'A strange place to find a body. On *that* beach.'

Dupont was right, of course, Bergerac realized. He should have paid more attention to the location. St Vimy's Bay was off the beaten track. It had little to offer sunbathers, swimmers or sailors. Only Mrs Awtry was likely to use it, and she was rarely on Jersey.

'How does Thornber earn his living?' Henri asked Belle.

'He doesn't. He's got a rich wife. Sometimes he takes parties of tourists out. But he can't make much out of that.'

The telephone cut into the conversation. Bergerac got up to answer it.

'Jim? This is Robert Wetherby.'

It was an effort to concentrate on what the clergyman was saying. Bergerac was also trying to listen to the conversation in the living room. The old man's timing was unfortunate.

'I hope I haven't disturbed you,' Wetherby went on. 'But I thought I should let you know. I may be a little late tomorrow. Perhaps half an hour. But I shall be coming.'

'Right. I'll see you then.'

Bergerac put down the phone. His head was buzzing with ideas, and none of them had anything to do with chess.

In the living room they were still talking about Thornber.

'Looks a bit like a pig,' Belle was saying with great solemnity. 'A pig with red bair and a heard. I mean red hair and a beard. And they say he's got a temper to match.'

'I wonder, Jim,' Henri said quietly, 'would you be able to . . .?'

'To make a few enquiries and let you know?' Bergerac grinned. 'You're a wily old devil, aren't you? I'll have to see him anyway.'

'International cooperation in the fight against crime,' Henri murmured piously. 'It'll be one of the keynotes in my speech at the conference.'

'But he may not be available for a while,' Bergerac said. 'Someone said he's gone down with scarlet fever.'

'Scarlet fever?' Susan said. 'I thought no one got that nowadays.'

'Oh, no,' Henri said, turning to her. 'We have a minor outbreak in France at this very moment. Nothing serious, but naturally the authorities are not going out of their way to publicize it. It's the sort of thing that could have a considerable effect on tourism.'

'You don't die of it, do you?' Bergerac asked.

'It yields to penicillin. But that's not the point. In the past it has had what you call a bad press.' He paused.

'They say it's moving northwards. The first reported cases were near the Spanish border. The most recent is in Le Mans.'

'Really?' Bergerac looked at the older man. 'Let me know if you hear any more about that, will you?'

Henri nodded. A slow smile spread over his face. 'Ah,' he said. 'I thought you might be interested.'

CHAPTER
7

A state of armed neutrality existed between Claude Yves and Chief Inspector Barney Crozier.

Yves, an overweight freelance reporter who was known behind his back as 'Michelin Man', derived an uncomplicated pleasure from baiting Crozier. On the first day of the conference, he sidled up to the Chief Inspector during the mid-morning break for coffee.

'How's the Body on the Beach today?' he wheezed. As usual, his chubby face was wreathed with gloom. 'Any news for my readers?'

'We're pursuing several lines of enquiry,' Crozier said tightly. 'As you very well know.'

'I hear you found something of his in the hotel safe. A notebook. Anything interesting?'

'I'm afraid I can't talk about that.'

'So you admit the Bureau has found a notebook belonging to Stroat.' Yves opened his shorthand pad. 'Good. Now about – '

'I admitted nothing of the sort,' Crozier snapped. 'You're putting words into my mouth.'

'Mrs Awtry said that an orchid was found on the body. Do the police attach any significance to that?'

'No comment.' Crozier glanced towards Prinknash, who was talking to an American judge on the other side of the conference hall. 'Now, if you'll excuse me, I must have a word with – '

'Detective Constable Goddard? Or Detective Constable Pettit? Yes, I noticed they were here. They've been keeping close to Sir Vernon, I see.' Yves' tiny eyes were bright with curiosity. 'You'd think the Stroat case would be stretching the Bureau's resources to their utmost. Yet here you are – three of you – lapping up all the goodies this international symposium has to offer. Nothing wrong with Sir Vernon, I hope?'

Charlie Hungerford pushed through the crowd and tapped Yves on the shoulder. Crozier seized his chance and escaped.

'Claude!' Hungerford beamed at the reporter. 'Going to give us a good write-up, I hope?'

'I'm only here for Sir Vernon,' Yves said. 'The nationals aren't going to be interested in what anyone else has to say.'

Hungerford frowned. 'That's a bit sweeping, isn't it? There are some very distinguished people here. Besides, you want to do your bit to put Jersey on the map, don't you? Having the conference here this year is good publicity for the island. My colleagues and I on the Tourism Committee are one hundred per cent in favour of it. It reinforces our safe, law-abiding image.'

Yves pursed his lips. 'I take your point, Deputy. You feel that at present Jersey's public image needs all the help it can get?'

'I didn't say that at all!' Hungerford throttled back his exasperation and went on in a quieter voice: 'You just look at the figures, Claude. Compare our incidence of crime against tourists with, say, Spain's or France's.'

'But no one looks at the figures. Your average holiday-maker looks at the newspaper. And what does he see? Elderly tourist brutally murdered on a Jersey beach. Over three days ago, and the police still haven't cleared it up.' Yves shook his head with grim satisfaction. 'Not the sort of place *I'd* choose for a holiday.'

'I happen to know,' Hungerford said stiffly, 'that the police are investigating a number of leads.'

'Oh, really? Would you care to be more specific?'

'I'm afraid I'm not at liberty to say.'

'You surprise me, Deputy. What about that speech you made in favour of freedom of information?'

'Well, you must see that was in quite a different context.' Hungerford edged away. 'Now, I must get back to my seat – '

'Just one more thing, Deputy. Could you comment on how the Tourism Committee plans to handle the outbreak of scarlet fever on the Island?'

'Eh?' Hungerford turned back to Yves. '*What* did you say? Scarlet fever?'

'You mean you haven't heard?' Yves made a note on his pad. 'It's not exactly going to encourage prospective tourists, I imagine. Especially families with young kids.'

'It's the first I've heard of it. Are you sure?'

Yves shrugged. 'It's early days, yet – only half a dozen cases so far. Three in St Helier and three in St Brelade.'

Hungerford and Yves joined the stream of people flowing back into the conference hall. Prinknash was chatting with the conference organizers on the stage. Yves had a seat at the side of the hall, near one of the exits. If it was at all possible, he always positioned himself near an exit at these affairs; it was rarely necessary to stay until the bitter end.

He sat down, expelling a breath of air like a deflating tyre. The chair creaked beneath his weight. He glanced at his watch. As a speaker, Prinknash had the reputation of being brisk and to the point. With a little luck, Yves thought, he might be out of the conference and into the bar by midday.

He noticed that Crozier had chosen a seat at the end of a row. The two DCs were standing unobtrusively in the gangways, covering both the flights of steps that led up to the stage. Yves wondered if he had hit the mark by accident, when he had asked Crozier if there was something wrong with Prinknash.

The buzz of conversation gradually subsided around him. Yves scribbled down a few notes that he might be able to use later. The comments – or rather the lack of them – from Hungerford and Crozier about the Stroat case might be worth a paragraph; one could hint at the police-inefficiency angle, always an old favourite; and of course the setting – the Third International Conference on Crime Prevention – gave an additional piquancy to the Bureau's failure to make progress with the murder.

But Prinknash was the real draw. Most of Yves' income derived from his work as a stringer for several mainland papers. They would be interested in what Prinknash had to say; but they wouldn't give a damn about the other speakers – a bunch of international nonentities.

The chairman of the conference organizers stood up to introduce his guest. Yves listened with half an ear to the biographical platitudes: '. . . distinguished war service . . . a brilliant career as a solicitor . . . an eloquent supporter of the police and the judiciary . . . well-known for his trench-ant views on crime and punishment . . . a rising politician . . . it is an open secret that he may soon be returning to the House of Commons . . .'

Prinknash ascended the rostrum. He carried a sheaf of notes, which he put down beside the microphone.

'Mr Chairman, ladies and gentlemen,' he began. 'That' – he tapped the papers before him – 'is the speech I intended to give you today. However, I hope you will forgive me if I speak to you not only without notes but also in an unusually autobiographical vein . . .'

Clever bugger, Yves thought without rancour. *He's trying to make them feel special.*

'. . . I hope you will not put this down to egocentricity on my part. It is merely that a recent experience of mine illustrates, in a nutshell, our current predicament. That predicament, of course, is not confined to Jersey and the

United Kingdom. Without any doubt whatsoever, it affects the entire free world.'

Prinknash looked slowly round the conference hall. *He's enjoying this*, Yves thought. *God, how I hate politicians*.

'For the last few weeks,' Prinknash resumed, 'I have been living under a sentence of death.'

A shocked murmur ran round the audience.

'A criminal syndicate has put a price on my head. As you know, I have made no secrets of my views in the past; and I have been able, in a small way, to be of assistance to the police. Now, it seems, the underworld has decided that I am not fit to live. In Britain, of course, we have rescinded the death penalty; we no longer have capital punishment; but the criminal fraternity – as I am learning to my cost – do not have such liberal views.

'I have received threatening phone calls and letters. I have been informed that I have less than a week to live. I know that the contract killer traced me to Jersey on the day of my arrival. He is here now. He may be in this very hall.'

The murmur had risen to a babble of surprise. *Damn good theatre*, Yves thought approvingly, as he scribbled furiously on his pad. *He's got ministerial potential, all right*. Prinknash held up his hand for silence.

'The police, of course, are doing their best to protect me. But their resources are already strained to breaking point. They cannot guarantee my safety, even in this room. For large periods of time – and much against their will, I may add – they have had to leave me completely unguarded.

'So it has come to this: the police, in this supposedly civilized society, can no longer ensure that law-abiding individuals may go in safety about their lawful business. They lack manpower; they lack material resources; and, most of all, they lack the supportive legal framework that once they had.

'As we all know, the published statistics confirm and

extend this depressing picture. Last year, thirty per cent of those convicted of robbery with violence . . .'

Yves pulled himself out of his chair. Prinknash was back on the rails now: this would be more or less his standard speech, advocating increased police powers and short, sharp shocks for all and sundry.

Two men and a woman were also leaving the hall. Yves recognized them as reporters from the mainland. Their departure confirmed his instinct: he needed to reach a phone. Prinknash's voice rumbled on.

Yves stumbled out of the hall and found himself in a corridor that led to the Hotel de Bretagne's reception area. There were several payphones in an alcove near the lifts.

He dialled the familiar London number. *Prinknash is a gambler*, it suddenly occurred to him. *He's playing for all or nothing.*

For the third time that day, Susan dialled Apley and Tuke's number. If she didn't get through this time, she would try the operator. Maybe there was a fault on the line.

The number rang at the other end. On the sixth ring someone picked up the phone.

'Hello? Can I help you?'

The voice belonged to a bored girl who had no apparent desire to help anyone.

'Is that Apley and Tuke?' Susan asked.

'One moment, I'll put you through.'

Silence descended on the other end of the line. Susan hated the way in which some switchboards consigned you to limbo while they were putting you through to an extension. The longer you waited, the more the suspicion grew that you had been permanently deserted; you felt you had been marooned in a corner of electronic ether that British Telecom subscribers reserved for unwanted callers.

After waiting for two minutes, Susan cut the connection. She punched the last-number-redial button and waited.

Eventually the switchboard operator condescended to answer.

'I've been trying to get through to Apley and Tuke,' Susan said. 'Is anyone there?'

'I think Mr Apley's away.'

'How about Mr Tuke?'

There was a long pause. Then the bored voice said, 'There isn't a Mr Tuke on my list.'

Susan took a breath. 'Well, isn't there a secretary or someone?'

'Not if no one's answering.'

'But there must be a secretary normally.'

'Well, *I* don't know, do I?' The girl was becoming irritated. 'I'm just a temp here, all right? There's dozens of firms in this building, and I'm expected to know everyone by name. I mean, it's stupid.'

'It's certainly is,' Susan agreed. 'Never mind, I'll write instead.'

The switchboard operator put the phone down without further ado.

'Susan,' Hobson said. 'Roger Rimmer phoned. He asked if you could get the Halkett Place lease to him today. His client's in a hurry.'

'All right, I'll have it biked over.' Susan hesitated. 'On second thoughts I'll go myself. I want a word with him.'

It was a relief to get out of the office. After the dinner party last night, she had a slight hangover: not enough to justify recourse to the Alka Seltzers in the medicine cupboard at the back of the office; but enough to make her thick-headed and irritable. Sometimes she was tempted to join Bergerac on the wagon.

She drove down to the office in Don Road. Rimmer was in the reception area, talking to his secretary, Elaine. His thin, dark face broke into a smile when he saw who it was.

68

Roger was usually pleased to see her – partly because she was an attractive woman, and partly because a lot of people asked their estate agent to recommend a solicitor when they were buying or selling a house.

'I'd offer you tea,' he said, 'but I've got a client due at 3.30. I'd keep him waiting if it wasn't rather important.'

'It doesn't matter. There was something I wanted to ask you: I'm trying to get hold of Apley and Tuke, but there seems to be no one at their London office. I wondered if you had another address for Mr Apley.'

Rimmer took her into his own room and consulted a filing cabinet. 'All our correspondence has been with an office in Albemarle Street. Is that where you tried to phone?'

Susan nodded. 'Do you know Apley personally?'

'Never met him. He needed a local solicitor to handle the bungalow lease, and someone in London referred him to me. Why do you want him?'

She grinned ruefully.'Need you ask? Mrs Elsted's had some more second thoughts. She'd now like to shorten the lease by a month.'

'I wish I could help you.'

'Never mind. I'll write them a letter.'

As Susan was leaving Rimmer's office, she nearly collided with an old man who was coming in. He murmured, 'I do beg your pardon,' and stepped aside to allow her to pass.

Susan paused on the threshold. The shock of white hair and the ancient tweed jacket jogged her memory.

'Wait a moment,' she said. 'It's Mr Wetherby, isn't it? I think we met just after Christmas. You were playing chess with Jim Bergerac.'

'With Jim? Of course, you're Jim's friend Susan, aren't you? I thought you looked familiar.' Wetherby beamed at her. 'I hope to have a game with him this evening.'

'Really? He . . . he didn't tell me he was planning to go out.'

The words were out of her mouth before she realized how revealing they were. But Wetherby appeared to have noticed nothing.

'If you see him beforehand,' he said, 'do emphasize that it doesn't matter if he's unable to come. I know he's very busy at present. I can always find someone to give me a game.' He smiled at her. 'But I mustn't keep you chattering. I gather you're a very busy woman yourself.'

He bobbed his head to her in a gesture of courtesy that belonged to another, politer generation, and slipped into Rimmer's office. Susan walked down the stairs.

It was only as she was climbing into the jeep that the penny dropped. Rimmer's important appointment must be with Mr Wetherby. The old clergyman was a strange client for such a blatantly ambitious solicitor.

Maybe she had misjudged Roger Rimmer all along. Maybe he was a closet philanthropist.

CHAPTER
8

A lonely figure in black sat, staring out to sea, in the garden of one of the cafés overlooking St Aubin's Bay. A tea tray was on the table. The tide was low, and many of the boats in the harbour were leaning at drunken angles. Seagulls swooped among their masts. Beyond the harbour was the fort, surrounded by sand like a stranded stone battleship. It was a peaceful scene; but the thoughts of the solitary customer were tense and feverish.

Today – definitely today. I'll finish the tea and go. There's no point in waiting any longer. Time is running out; for all we know it has already run out. Always the risk of someone recognizing me. Don't think of that possibility. I wish I didn't feel so bloody awful. Thoughts out of control; but they always come back to him. The old bastard. Thinks he's God, that's his trouble; it always has been. Why did the fool have to be so stupid? I don't really want to hurt him, even now. But I shall, if I have to. Can't afford to be sentimental. He's mad, he must be. It's his fault, anyone can see that. He's forcing me to do this. They should have shut him up in an asylum years ago.

The harbour formed an irregular quadrilateral. The natural formation of the coastline contributed two of the sides. The others consisted of stone jetties, one of which ended with the lighthouse that marked the narrow mouth of the harbour. The customer idly followed the progress of a man in a leather jacket, who was walking slowly along one of the jetties.

There was something familiar about the way he walked. The customer shrugged and picked up the teapot. The stream of liquid trickled into the cup. The customer's eyes returned to the man on the jetty.

He had stopped for a chat with an elderly fisherman in a blue jersey. The fisherman was pointing out something in the harbour. The man pointed, too. You could almost hear him saying, 'What? You mean that one?'

The tea reached the rim of the cup and, unnoticed, spilled over and flooded the saucer. The customer swore as hot water splashed on bare skin.

It's the copper! Bergerac! And he's looking at the Golden Rialto. *What the hell's he doing? He can't know anything – it's impossible. Maybe I'm hallucinating . . . Maybe I'm going mad . . .*

The customer stood up, dropped a five-pound note on the table and walked quickly away from the café.

Bergerac swung the Triumph into the tarmac drive of the Orchid Factory. Instead of parking by the display house, he followed the road round to the left. It led him through the belt of trees to the front of a substantial house.

The building was shaped like a capital E without the central prong. The drive described a circle round a fountain in the hollow of the E. The fountain was built of weathered stone; three cherubs were arranged in improbable postures on the edge of the basin.

He parked the car beside a rust-stained VW Beetle with a sun-bleached notice, DOCTOR ON CALL, permanently attached to its windscreen. The front door was approached by a long flight of steps. The house's design suggested that its nineteenth-century architect had an unwholesome fascination for Renaissance Italy. Like the gardens, it was in immaculate condition.

The door opened before he reached it. On the threshold stood a woman with short, iron-grey hair and a determined chin.

She glanced down at him. Then the chin rose contemptuously. 'Yes?'

72

'States Police, madam. Detective Sergeant Bergerac.'

'I find it difficult to believe that that is a police car.'

Bergerac resisted the temptation to tell her that Chief Inspector Crozier had the same problem. He showed her his warrant card. She made no move to invite him in.

'You're Mrs Thornber, I take it?'

She gave the barest nod.

'I wonder if I could have a word with you. It's about the murder of Julian Stroat.'

'Never met the man.'

'He visited the Orchid Factory on Friday, the day before his death. He bought an "*Odontioda* Mary Thornber". May I come in?'

'If you must.'

Mrs Thornber retreated into the hall. Large and cool, it was floored with black and white flagstones like a gigantic chessboard. She took up her position by an immense marble fireplace. There were chairs grouped around it, but she made no move to offer him a seat.

'I talked to two of your staff on Saturday,' Bergerac said. 'Mrs Le Vare and Dan Fisher. It was Fisher who actually served Stroat.'

'I know. They told me.'

'Were you aware that Sir Vernon Prinknash was another customer on that afternoon?'

She nodded.

'Do you know him?'

'Only by reputation.'

Bergerac wondered if she was always as laconic at this. 'When did you find out that he'd called?'

'Prinknash? Late on Friday afternoon. I made the arrangements for air-freighting his order.'

'Where did you send the orchids?'

'To London. They were for Lady Prinknash. Sergeant, I fail to see what this has to do with the death of the man Stroat.'

73

Bergerac met her eyes. 'Just checking. It may not have anything to do with it. I'm trying to find out if there *is* a connection.'

She sniffed and said, 'I suppose you know your own business,' in a manner that implied she supposed the opposite.

'Was your husband at the Orchid Factory that afternoon?'

The chin rose again. 'As a matter of fact, he was.'

There was a note of caution in her voice that had not been there before. She was still faintly hostile, Bergerac realized, but now she was also wary. Maybe Jack Thornber aroused her protective instinct.

For the first time she volunteered more information without waiting for him to prompt her with another question. 'He's not normally there – he has his own business to look after. But sometimes he helps out if we're short-staffed, or if I have to be away.'

Bergerac moved on to the real purpose of his visit. 'I'd like to see him, if I may.'

'I'm afraid you can't,' Mrs Thornber said sharply. She hesitated before adding, in a less aggressive tone, 'He's gone down with scarlet fever, of all things. The doctor's with him now. I . . . I know for a fact that he didn't meet Stroat on Friday.'

A door closed, somewhere above their heads. There were soft footsteps on the landing.

'You talked about it later?' Bergerac said.

'Naturally – when Mrs Le Vare told us about your visit. So you see there's no point in your seeing my husband even if the doctor permitted it.'

'Permitted what?'

Bergerac and Mrs Thornber looked up. A heavily-built man in a baggy grey suit was coming slowly down the stairs.

'Hello, Jim,' he said. 'Thought I recognized your car.'

Dr Fender was a long-established GP. At one time Bergerac had been among his patients.

'How's Jack?' Mrs Thornber asked abruptly.

'He's beginning to mend. The penicillin's doing its job, and his temperature's dropping. But he's had a bad go of it.'

'Is there anything I can do?'

'Just carry on with the fever regime.' Fender moved towards the front door, talking over his shoulder; Mrs Thornber followed him. 'Keep him in bed, lots of fluids, light diet: you know the sort of thing. I'll look in again tomorrow.'

'Doctor?'

Fender paused at the door.

'What is it, Jim?'

'Is there any medical reason why I shouldn't have a word with him?'

Bergerac put a faint stress on the word 'medical'. The doctor glanced at Mrs Thornber.

'Mr Thornber should avoid unnecessary excitement at present,' he said.

'I wouldn't overtire him – just a few minor questions; they relate to a murder enquiry.'

'Stroat?' Fender grunted. 'Bad business, that. Urgent, is it?'

'It might be. Difficult to say.'

'I've already told Sergeant Bergerac that my husband can't help him,' Mrs Thornber interrupted. 'So the question doesn't arise.'

'But I need to confirm that for myself,' Bergerac said. 'I'm sure you understand.'

The doctor shrugged his massive shoulders. 'Five minutes' gentle conversation wouldn't hurt him, Mrs Thornber. Might even cheer him up – among other things, he's suffering from boredom.'

She nodded unwillingly. 'He's never been a good patient.'

Bergerac pressed home his advantage. 'It's nothing to worry about – just for the record. Otherwise I'll have to come back another time.'

'Oh, very well.'

Mrs Thornber opened the front door. The sunlight beyond created an unflattering silhouette of her profile.

Fender jingled his car keys. 'I'm off to see young Fisher. You heard he'd gone down with it?'

'Yes – I presume he caught it from my husband.'

'How did Mr Thornber get it?' Bergerac asked.

'I don't know,' Fender said. 'It's highly contagious. It can be transmitted by a patient or a carrier – or even through contaminated milk. If you haven't had scarlet fever yourself, I wouldn't advise you to get too close to him.'

When the doctor had gone, Mrs Thornber escorted Bergerac to a first-floor bedroom that overlooked the front of the house; it was large, airy and very tidy.

Jack Thornber was sitting up in bed, reading a newspaper. He was a thickset man, who looked some years younger than his wife. Above his beard, the cheeks were covered with a rash of tiny spots on a flushed base. His curly, reddish-gold hair clashed with the purple duvet.

Mrs Thornber advanced into the room. Bergerac, mindful of Fender's warning, lingered on the threshold.

'Who's this?' Thornber demanded hoarsely, dropping the newspaper on the bed.

'Sergeant Bergerac,' his wife said. She began to plump up her husband's pillows. 'Fender said he could ask you a few questions about that man Stroat. Just for a minute.'

'I won't keep you long, sir,' Bergerac said. 'Your wife tells me you don't remember seeing Stroat when he visited the Orchid Factory on Friday.'

Mrs Thornber had her back to the door. She was refilling

the invalid's glass from a jug of what looked like lemon barley water.

Thornber shook his head. 'We were very busy. I didn't notice him.' His eyes slid away from Bergerac's and he took a long swallow from the glass. 'Bloody throat's killing me,' he said to his wife.

'Then don't talk so much.'

'But you talked to Sir Vernon Prinknash?' Bergerac said.

'Briefly. He asked me about some orchids he wanted to send to his wife.'

'You knew who he was?'

Thornber nodded. He moaned faintly and, to Bergerac's ears at least, rather theatrically.

'Have you finished, Sergeant?' Mrs Thornber said fiercely.

'I won't be long. Had you met Sir Vernon before, sir?'

'No.'

'I understand you were talking to him in the Marine Bar of the Hotel de Bretagne at Friday lunchtime.'

'You never told me that,' his wife said.

Thornber moved restlessly against the pillows. 'Because it didn't seem very significant,' he said irritably, scratching his beard. His eyes returned to Bergerac. 'I thought you meant had I met him before Friday. I was at the Bretagne and someone told him I was connected with the Orchid Factory. He came over to ask whether we were open and what sort of stuff we had in stock. So I told him, and he came. That's all there is to it. But I'd like to know who's been spying on me . . . Anyway, what's so important about Prinknash?'

'That's what I wanted to know,' Mrs Thornber said.

'I think that's everything,' Bergerac said smoothly; he was under no obligation to answer their questions. 'Thank you both for your time.' *If not for your courtesy and helpfulness*, he added to himself.

Mrs Thornber saw him out of the house.

'Oh, by the way,' Bergerac said as she opened the front door. 'What does your husband actually do?'

'He has a boat,' Mrs Thornber said. 'He charters it to tourists and so forth – usually to complete duffers who want to pretend they're sailors.'

'The *Golden Rialto*?'

She nodded curtly.

'So he's away quite a lot?'

'Occasionally. Look here, Sergeant, what is this? Why are you asking all these damn-fool questions?'

'It's part of the job, Mrs Thornber. In a murder enquiry, ninety-nine per cent of the information we get is useless.'

'In your case, I imagine the percentage is even higher.'

Bergerac smiled. He hoped it wasn't obvious to her that he had lost his temper. 'The point is, we're not in a position to know what's useful and what isn't until afterwards.'

'And when is that?'

'When we've found the killer.'

Susan could hear him on the phone.

'No joy, Barney. She's about as soft and cuddly as heavy-duty sandpaper, and he's not much better . . . No, nothing concrete . . . All right, I'll see you tomorrow.'

He put down the phone and picked up his jacket.

Susan looked up from her book. 'Going off to play chess with your clerical chum?'

'Oh, come on, Sue.'

Their eyes met.

'I saw him today at a solicitor's,' she went on. 'Maybe he's going to leave you all his money.'

She knew that the sarcasm was worse than childish: it was ineffectual. Jim had decided to go out. There was nothing she could say to change his mind.

He slammed the door as he left the house. That was some satisfaction.

*

The chess club met in the upstairs room of Odell's wine bar in Halkett Place. The wine bar was struggling to survive, which was why the club met there on the first and third Tuesdays of every month.

The proprietor was willing to go almost to any lengths to attract customers, even chess players. Chess players added intellectual distinction to an establishment; but no one could claim they were big spenders. Many of them could last for hours on a single drink. But they filled the tables and created the illusion that the place was busy.

The club was not really a club at all, but an informal group of acquaintances, all of whom enjoyed the occasional game of chess. The skills of the players varied widely. There was little organization: the club did not go in for league tables and competitions; you played with whom you wanted and how you wanted.

Bergerac was a few minutes late. He was surprised to find that Wetherby was not already there. He chatted to other members, refusing several offers of a game. He began to wonder if fate was punishing him for slamming the door on Susan.

He gave it half an hour and then went downstairs to the payphone. It was unlike Wetherby to forget an appointment; perhaps he was ill. The number for the Halton House Home for Retired Clergy was in the book.

The secretary answered the call. Bergerac explained why he was phoning. She thought Wetherby was out; he hadn't been in for supper. She phoned up to his room, but there was no answer. Halton House was run along relaxed lines: residents were not required to sign in and out.

'It's probably another emergency,' the secretary said.

'An emergency? What do you mean?'

'Robert still does a lot of pastoral work – he's very popular locally. One of our more active residents. People are always phoning him up with a crisis.' Her voice warmed as she spoke about him. 'Sometimes we hardly see him for weeks at a time.'

Bergerac thanked her and put down the phone. It was another unexpected sidelight on Wetherby. Bergerac had known that the old man occasionally took services, filling in for the overworked clergy in the area. Now it seemed that he was also a one-man branch of the social services.

Upstairs there were a number of people who would give Bergerac a game; but he decided not to stay. It would be better to try to patch things up with Susan. He left the wine bar and turned into Burrard Street. The car was in the car park behind the Odeon, at the far end of James Street.

At this time of the evening there were few cars and fewer pedestrians. It was a soft, mild night. He had left the car near one of the emergency exits from the cinema. As he bent to unlock the car door, he heard a hinge squeal behind him. A bar of light from the exit ran across the asphalt and up the side of the car.

He had no warning. It happened in a matter of seconds. The events followed so fast upon one another that they seemed simultaneous, rather than arranged in a sequence.

There was a flurry of footsteps. He began to straighten up. There was a rush of displaced air against his cheek.

Something hit his head, an inch or two above the left ear. The pain enveloped him. His vision blurred, and his consciousness seemed to darken, as though someone had masked it with black chiffon.

His body slumped down the side of the car. Someone grunted. The Triumph's door felt cool and slightly moist against his cheek. An agonizing pain shot through his left side, and he heard himself scream.

A car engine was revving in low gear. Bergerac's head rested by one of the Triumph's wheels. He could see underneath his own car – underneath dozens of cars. A pair of headlights dazzled his eyes. He looked away.

At precisely the same time, a fold of dark material

brushed against his face. It smelled faintly musty. He would not have seen it at all if he had not turned his head. It was irrelevant, he thought vaguely. At present, only the pain was important.

More running footsteps. The headlights swept away. The bar of light from the emergency exit shrank and disappeared. Metal clanked against metal.

Then, at the centre of the darkness, there was only pain.

CHAPTER
9

'What the hell are you doing here?' Crozier said. 'You look as if you should be in bed.'

'That's what Susan said.' Bergerac sat down in the chair in front of the desk. 'Anyway, shouldn't you be at the Bretagne?'

'The conference can start without me. Goddard can tell me what Henri Dupont is saying. You've seen a doctor?'

'They patched me up in Casualty last night.'

Crozier frowned. 'If you ask me, they should have kept you in for observation.'

Bergerac shrugged, which made him wince. 'They wanted to. I had to promise I'd see someone today.'

'Dennis is downstairs.' Crozier picked up the internal phone and punched a number. 'You can see him as soon as he's free.'

'Can't it wait, Barney? I've got a hundred and one – '

'Dennis? Can you have a look at Jim Bergerac when you've finished?' The phone crackled in Crozier's hand. 'Head injury and a knife wound . . . No, I quite agree. He's a fool.' Crozier put down the handset. 'Half an hour, in his office,' he said to Bergerac. 'And if he wants you off-duty, you go off-duty. Is that clear?'

'Yes, Chief Inspector.'

'You think there's a connection between the Stroat case and the rough stuff last night?'

'No evidence one way or the other.'

'How did it happen?'

'Unless it was a random mugger, someone must have

followed me from Susan's, and seen me park behind the Odeon. A performance was about to start – there were a lot of people around. Or maybe he had to park his own car. In any case, he didn't have a crack at me before I went to Odell's. He went to the cinema instead. One of the exits was just by my car. And I reckon he waited there, with the door ajar.'

'You might have been gone for hours.'

'It was a gamble, all right, but it damn nearly came off. As soon as I came back, he nipped out and hit me over the head. Then he started to finish me off with a knife. But luckily a car came into the car park, so he had to retreat.'

'We've checked out the cinema, I presume?'

'Goddard went round last night. A full-capacity house. Seven exits, and only the one at the front was manned. Our friend had at least thirty minutes to play with before the alarm was raised.'

'Neat,' Crozier said with reluctant admiration. 'The only real gamble was whether or not he got you. He didn't take much personal risk.'

'I should have reacted faster,' Bergerac said. 'There's no excuse.'

'Don't be stupid, man.'

'Sometimes I think I'm getting too old for this.'

'You can save your self-pity for the doctor,' Crozier said tartly. 'Your last medical report gave you the second fastest reflexes in the Bureau.'

'Who's the fastest?'

'Willy Pettit. But don't tell him. He's bumptious enough as it is.' He looked at his watch. 'I'd better put on an appearance at the Bretagne.'

'Tough going, is it?' Bergerac said.

'It'd be a damn sight easier if Prinknash had kept his mouth shut yesterday. I wish to God he'd go home. You seen the nationals today? He's front-page news.'

83

'He's a clever man. In a way, you've got to hand it to him: he's no coward.'

Crozier snorted. 'Then I've got Hungerford and Claude Yves breathing down my neck.' He imitated Michelin Man's wheezing voice: '"How's the Body on the Beach today?" And Charlie's got yet another bee in his bonnet: this scarlet fever business. The next thing we'll know, his precious Committee will want the Bureau to arrest all germs on sight.'

The last sentence did something to restore Crozier's good humour; he so rarely made a joke that he was rather proud of it when one slipped out, almost by accident.

He walked through the main office with Bergerac. Peggy hailed them as they passed.

'Sergeant Tuffnell is on the line.'

'You take it, Jim,' Crozier said. 'And I just hope it's good news.'

It was good news as far as fifty-three individuals, mainly resident in London and the Home Counties, were concerned. It was bad news for the Bureau des Etrangers.

'We traced Stroat's safe deposits,' Gordie Tuffnell said. 'And I've talked to all his victims. The report's on its way, but I thought you'd like a preview. You know, I felt like a bloody Father Christmas. They were all so relieved – even the ones we had to collar.'

'Many of those?' Bergerac asked.

'No. Stroat was small-time, really.' Tuffnell sighed, as if bored by the parade of human frailty he had been forced to witness. 'Bored housewives with jealous husbands. Shop assistants with their hands in the till. Suburban mothers who didn't want the neighbours to know that little Johnny was inside for dealing coke. Businessmen who took a tart to bed and found that she was a he with a camera.'

'So where does it leave us?'

'We're happy enough, but I doubt if you will be.'

'They've got alibis?'

'Every last one. Anyway, most of them aren't the type to begin with. You know the sort: they think a garrotte is what Good Queen Bess danced with the Earl of Leicester.'

'Didn't know you were a historian, Gordie.'

'There's a lot you don't know, Jim. Including who killed Stroat. I'm sorry.'

'So am I. But thanks.'

'There was one other thing,' Tuffnell said. 'Nothing to do with Stroat, but you might be interested. Just a bit of gossip, really – I got it from one of my snouts last night. He said he'd heard a rumour that Veldman's somewhere in North Africa.'

'How reliable is he?'

'Fifty per cent, maybe? He's one of these blokes who mean well, but he's got the critical intelligence of a garden worm. According to his source, Veldman's on her uppers and looking for work. But for all we know that's just disinformation. I wouldn't put anything past Veldman.'

'No,' Bergerac said.

'You okay? You sound a bit under the weather.'

'I'm fine, Gordie.'

They said goodbye. Bergerac put the phone down and sat at his desk, staring into space. His head and his side were throbbing. Around him, people chattered and phones rang. He felt insulated from the rest of the Bureau, as though he were enclosed in a cage of soundproof glass.

It was Wednesday morning – over four days since Mrs Awtry had discovered Stroat's body. Identifying him had been their only solid achievement. They were no closer to finding out who had killed him than they had been at the beginning.

'Jim? Jim?'

A hand touched his shoulder, and he glanced up. Peggy was looking down at him, with an anxious expression on her face.

'You look as if you were miles away,' she said. 'Are you all right?'

'Everyone keeps asking me that,' he said wearily. 'It's the bandage round the head that does it. A universal magnet for human sympathy.'

'You don't look well. Dr Lejeune phoned: he's ready for you now. And about time, too.'

Bergerac went downstairs to the doctor's office, which was conveniently situated near the mortuary. Dennis Lejeune was filling in a post-mortem form; he nodded at a chair and sneezed.

'Be with you in a moment.' He was an untidy, heavily bearded man in his fifties. 'Bloody forms.'

The ticking of the clock on the wall and the scratching of Lejeune's biro filled the silence. There was a large, empty glass ashtray on the desk. Lejeune signed his name with a flourish and threw down the pen.

'Let's have a look at the head first.'

The thick fingers were surprisingly gentle as they removed the bandage and probed the shallow wound beneath.

'You got this stitch at the General Hospital?' Lejeune said.

'That's right.'

'They made a good job of it.' Lejeune was probably aware that he was causing pain, for he continued to chat, as if to provide a distraction. 'They're over the moon at present. Someone's promised them a seven-figure donation.'

'Who's it from?'

'Anonymous. Maybe it's that chap Prinknash. He's meant to be rolling.'

'Not Prinknash. He's – ' Bergerac bit his lip to stop himself from crying out. 'He's not the sort to avoid publicity. What do you think of the wound?'

'Blunt instrument?'

'Something like a spanner, I think.'

Lejeune grunted. 'Lucky it wasn't a bit lower.'

Bergerac tried to turn the conversation to someone else's problems: 'I see you've given up smoking again.'

'As a result I've got the worst cold I've had for years; I've put on three pounds I don't need; and my bowels are shot to pieces. Makes you wonder, doesn't it?'

He put another dressing on the head and replaced the bandage.

'Get your shirt off, and up on the couch.'

He whistled when he saw what the knife had done. 'Hit a rib, I suppose. And just as well.'

'That close?'

'That close. But you'll mend.' Lejeune hesitated. 'It wouldn't do you any harm to have a few days' peace and quiet.'

'Except it wouldn't be peace and quiet.'

'No – you'd be worrying yourself sick and imagining you're indispensable.'

'Let me see how it goes.'

'All right. But I'll tell Barney Crozier to pack you off on sick leave if you show the slightest sign of – '

'I won't, Dennis. You'll see.' Bergerac quickly changed the subject. 'I expect you're brushing up on scarlet fever?'

'Nothing to brush up,' Lejeune said. 'It's really just a streptococcal infection with a bad reputation. These days it's nothing that antibiotics and bed-rest can't cope with.'

'The Tourism Committee aren't very happy. The press has got hold of it.'

Lejeune shrugged. 'Admittedly it seems to be a slightly unusual strain. I was talking to old Fender last night. There's a lack of circumoral pallor, for one thing, and the blistering for another.'

'Care to translate?'

'Normally the rash doesn't affect the area round the mouth. But it does here. And there's some separation of the layers of affected skin. Nothing to make a song-and-dance about. Just – well, interesting. Laymen never realize that most routine medicine gets dreadfully repetitive: it's boring. Fender's delighted. He's going to write to the *Lancet*.'

'I saw one of his patients yesterday: Jack Thornber. He wasn't very happy.'

Lejeune began to redo the bandage. 'Surly man, lovely boat. I've met him once or twice at the Yacht Club. Do you know his boat? The *Golden Rialto*. I wish I could afford something like that.' The doctor fumbled in his jacket pocket, looking for a packet of cigarettes that wasn't there. 'But Thornber's a devious sort of chap,' he went on. 'Did you know he didn't trust Fender's diagnosis? Called in a second opinion, privately. Went behind Fender's back. Not that it did him any good – the second opinion was precisely the same as the first, right down to the antibiotics that were prescribed. All right, you can put your shirt on, now.'

Bergerac sat up. Getting his arms into the sleeves of his shirt was a painful process, though he tried to conceal the fact from Lejeune. He swung his legs off the couch and stood up.

Lejeune was back at his desk, scribbling on a prescription pad.

'What's that for?' Bergerac asked.

'Parahypon. They're mild painkillers. You're going to need some help if you want to pretend you can't feel a thing.'

Bergerac thanked him and went back upstairs. For no apparent reason, he felt better for seeing Lejeune. On his desk he found a message from Peggy, asking him to phone the secretary of the Halton House Home for Retired Clergy.

The message jolted his memory, and he remembered that Wetherby had failed to turn up last night. He would have expected the old man to ring today. But why should the secretary want to get in touch with him?

He dialled the number. The secretary picked up the phone on the first ring.

'I'm so glad you've phoned. I just don't know what to do.'

'What's up?'

'It's Robert Wetherby. I think ... I think he's disappeared.'

Susan knew she shouldn't have called Bergerac a Dumb Rambo.

And it was unfortunate that he had misunderstood her passing reference to *Boy's Own* heroes – or, rather, that he had understood it all too well.

But he made her so angry. The call from the hospital last night had shaken her up more than she cared to admit. Seeing Jim – with that ridiculous bandage above the pale, strained face – had made it even worse. All right, taking risks was part of the job; she had become resigned to that. But going on duty as though nothing had happened was worse than stupid: it was selfish, because it affected her as well as him. A knot of tension had taken up residence in the pit of her stomach. She wondered bleakly if he imagined that she enjoyed worrying about him.

There was nothing she could do about it. She fought the temptation to contact the Bureau. If she could talk to Jim, she told herself, she could get a better idea of how he was really feeling. She might even get around to apologizing for what she had said. On the other hand, she might learn nothing. Bergerac disliked personal calls at work at the best of times, and he would probably think she was playing the nagging wife.

So she tried to immerse herself in work. The frustration's piled up. Apley and Tuke failed to phone, but Mrs Elsted did; and she talked about the Brazilian niece and Brighton shops for twenty minutes. Susan rang the bungalow and let the phone ring until the operator came on the line to tell her she was wasting her time. She even called at the bungalow on her way to do a survey in St Martin. No one answered the door. Net curtains shrouded the rooms from prying eyes, and the garage was locked.

The temptation grew stronger. The knot of tension tightened. When she got back to the office just before lunch, she went straight to the phone.

'Jim's gone out, I'm afraid,' Peggy said. 'Somewhere in Gorey, I think. Can I take a message?'

'No, don't bother. Peggy, how did he look?'

'Well, to be perfectly honest, I thought he needed tucking up in bed with a hot-water bottle. He's very pale, Susan. And he moves as though he were made of eggshells.'

'Damn him,' Susan muttered angrily.

'Yes, dear.' Peggy understood immediately. 'My husband was just the same. He had pneumonia once, and I remember I had to practically *chain* him to the bed to keep him there. I suppose men don't like feeling inadequate, so they just pretend they aren't. It's so childish.'

'When you see him, can you . . . ?' Susan's voice trailed away. 'No, it doesn't matter. Thanks, Peggy.'

She put the phone down. The knot in her stomach grew tighter and tighter.

Lunch was being served at Halton House. The secretary saw Bergerac standing in the doorway of the dining room. She quickly rose from her seat and followed him into the hall.

'I didn't recognize you for a moment,' she said, as she opened the door to her little office. She was a small woman, whose movements reminded Bergerac of a sparrow looking for worms on a lawn. 'That bandage makes you look quite different. Are you all right?'

'Fine,' Bergerac said grimly. 'Any news of Robert?'

She shook her head. Her normally placid face was drawn

with anxiety. 'I followed your advice and contacted the local police. They're going to send someone round.'

'So there's nothing more? He just vanished yesterday, sometime before supper?'

'I've found out a little more.' The secretary sat down; Bergerac was glad to follow suit. 'His wallet and his jacket are still in his room. And I've talked to all the residents since I phoned you. Mr Jones thought that Robert had an evensong lined up at Grouville. But when I rang the Rector, he said he'd taken it himself because his sore throat was better.'

'So where was he last seen?'

'In the garden.' Her shoulders twitched. 'As usual. He'd been into St Helier, to see his solicitor, I think, and he got back just as we were finishing tea. He was working down by the gates, so Mr Hubert said. But Mr Hubert isn't . . . well, he's getting on a bit. He'll be ninety-three in July. Our oldest resident.'

'Did he see anything?' Bergerac asked.

'I really don't know. He was sitting on the bench that overlooks the drive; it gets the sun in the late afternoon. Personally I think he was asleep. Some of them have very vivid dreams, you know; and the older ones, poor lambs, often find it hard to distinguish between dreams and reality. And bearing in mind Mr Hubert's brand of Anglo-Catholicism, I wouldn't be surprised if he *did* imagine it.'

The bandage round Bergerac's head seemed to be getting tighter, and he was finding it difficult to concentrate.

'I don't quite understand how the Anglo-Catholicism fits in.'

'I'm sorry.' The secretary rubbed her forehead. 'I'm not making myself clear, am I? Mr Hubert believes that priests should take a vow of celibacy – as they do in the Roman Catholic church. He's also a great advocate of monasticism. So when he said that Robert walked out of the gates, arm-in-arm with a Roman Catholic nun, I naturally wondered if he'd been dreaming.'

'A nun?' Bergerac said faintly.

'Yes. Mr Hubert was really rather shocked. "Just as if they were husband and wife," he kept saying. "Just as if they were husband and wife."'

CHAPTER
10

Bergerac was pleased to notice that he hardly winced at all as he climbed out of the Triumph.

During the day, the pain had come in waves. It hadn't been so bad in the lulls between the onslaughts. This time, he hoped, the lull was going to be permanent.

Maybe the painkillers had helped, or the distraction of work. Or it could simply be that he was getting better. Whatever the reason, Bergerac felt almost normal as he walked into the Hotel de Bretagne.

The Marine Bar was full of conference delegates, tanking up before the rigours of dinner. Anne-Marie had gathered a circle of middle-aged admirers round the piano. Henri sat alone at a corner table, nursing an enormous glass of sparkling wine. He was looking unusually smart in a dark-blue, double-breasted suit.

His eyebrows shot up when he saw the bandage. 'You look like a pirate, my dear Jim. A damaged pirate. Crozier told me about last night. Are you all right?'

'Everyone asks me that.' Bergerac sat down in the empty chair beside Dupont's and refused the offer of a drink. 'I'm fine. How did it go?'

'This morning? As well as could be expected. I read my colleague's speech. Then people asked me questions I could not answer because I know nothing about surveillance techniques for international terrorists. Thank God.' He looked at his watch. 'I – ah – have a date, so we haven't got long. Tell me – what exactly happened last night?'

Bergerac described the attack as briefly as possible. He

93

also mentioned his abortive meeting with Wetherby and the fact that Wetherby had disappeared. Then Dupont asked him how he had got on with Thornber.

When Bergerac had finished, there was a short silence. Anne-Marie was somewhere over the rainbow, way up high, probably hoping to find the pot of gold.

'Difficult,' Henri said at last. It was not a helpful remark.

'The big problem is the absence of firm connections,' Bergerac said 'There seem to be links but maybe we're fooling ourselves.'

'How do you mean?'

'Stroat is killed on a beach. A killer is after Prinknash, one of Stroat's potential victims. Prinknash knows Thornber, who has a boat. Mrs Thornber grows orchids. Stroat buys one, Prinknash buys several. Robert Wetherby tells me that Stroat's orchid came from Mrs Thornber's place. Last night, Robert fails to meet me, and I'm nearly killed as I return from the rendezvous. You're interested in Thornber because you're looking for a smuggling route. There seem to be connections but each affair could be entirely separate.'

Henri coughed. 'You've left something out: Thornber has scarlet fever, and so have people in France.'

Bergerac leant forward. 'Have you heard any more about that?'

Henri nodded. 'I had a phone call just before you came. It appears that our *fièvre scarlatine* has some abnormal features: blistering is one; and a rash around the mouth is another. I am told that this makes it a unique strain. Could you find out – ?'

'I already have.' Bergerac grinned. 'One of our doctors knows Thornber's GP. And yes, the GP noticed the same symptoms.'

'That,' Henri said with great seriousness, 'is progress.'

'There's more?'

'We've traced it through Spain to Tangier. The first recorded cases were in Casablanca.'

'Morocco? Are you sure?'

'As much as one can be. Why?'

Bergerac shrugged. 'Just an idea. Let me check it out first.'

'And there is even more,' Henri went on. 'I think I have a connection for you.' He sipped his wine, prolonging the moment of triumph. 'My deputy reports that there has been a case in Carteret itself. A woman who owns a café near the harbour. A woman of a certain reputation, if you understand me.'

Bergerac was in no mood for guessing games. 'I'm not sure that I do.'

Henri raised his eyebrows at this example of British obtuseness. 'It is said that the woman has a lover. A rich English sailor, who often spends a day or two in Carteret. The man has a red beard.'

They sat in silence for a moment. Bergerac's mouth was dry: that was a common physical reaction when he sensed a breakthrough in a case. He had a feeling that the breakthrough was even more significant than Henri realized. But the idea was too fragile to be mentioned. It was only guesswork; a breath of criticism could blow it away. He hugged it to himself.

'My superiors,' Henri continued, 'have given me permission to leave the conference early, so that I may pursue enquiries on the spot. I leave tomorrow morning. I wonder, would you . . .?'

'I would,' Bergerac said. 'If we can tie Thornber in with St Vimy's Bay – '

'Henri!'

Startled, Bergerac looked up. He had a fleeting impression of someone swathed in black and smelling strongly of mothballs. His mind cleared and he fought back the desire to laugh. Belle Young was dressed for a night on the town.

The Frenchman was already standing, pulling back a chair for Belle. 'My dear, you look ravishing,' he murmured. If he wasn't sincere, he was putting on an excellent imitation.

'It's my little black dress,' Belle said, flushing with pleasure at the compliment. 'I've had it for years. It never goes out of fashion. I'm a little early.' She looked at Bergerac with a marked lack of enthusiasm. 'What are *you* doing here?'

'Just passing through,' Bergerac said hastily, pushing back his chair.

He found it difficult to take his eyes off Belle. Usually she wore a faded fisherman's smock over baggy, oil-stained trousers, which made her appearance this evening all the more striking. Her hair was pinned up; there was make-up, inexpertly applied, on her face; she wore earrings and a necklace that looked as if they had been inherited from her grandmother; and the black dress, with its long, full skirt and its lowcut bodice, would not have looked out of place in a museum.

'A large pink gin?' Henri suggested caressingly. 'We must have something while we discuss where we shall eat.'

'I'll be off, then,' Bergerac said awkwardly. 'I'll phone you later, Henri.'

'Eh?'

'About that other matter.'

'Ah, yes.' Dupont glanced down at Belle. 'But I may not be here. Still, you can always leave a message for me.'

'Goodbye, Jim,' Belle said, ready to be friendly now that she was sure of his departure. 'Give my love to Susan.'

Bergerac walked away from them. Anne-Marie was playing 'Sixteen Going on Seventeen'. He looked back over his shoulder, intending to wave, but Henri and Belle were already absorbed in one another. Bergerac knew that he had been excluded. He tried to convince himself that there was a comic element in what he had just seen. He imagined describing the pair of them to Susan: Henri like a retired gangster with a French accent; Belle in her finery like a pantomime dame; and, between them, an improbable mutual attraction, apparently fuelled by a rich mixture of pink gin, Armagnac and Spanish sparkling wine. Grey-haired lovers were meant to be funny, weren't they?

But these two merely made him envious.

Conferences and cases came and went, but paperwork was eternal.

Barney Crozier initialled the sixth report on his desk and reached for the seventh. He yawned and rubbed his eyes; he didn't need to look in the mirror to know that they were red-rimmed. He swallowed a mouthful of lukewarm coffee. Because of the conference, he had had to work late last night; and he would have to do the same tomorrow. Thank God it was only a three-day affair. Some conferences went on for a week. Senior officers, with their bizarre enthusiasm for conferences and courses of all descriptions, generally failed to realize that you still needed time to do the routine work. Nevertheless, they expected the Bureau to function as normal.

The seventh report was on the Stroat case. Bergerac had added Tuffnell's information. Crozier skimmed through it, his depression growing. It was a messy, inconclusive business, with the additional complication of political ramifications. If only Prinknash would stop striking well-publicized poses and go back to London.

Crozier noticed that Bergerac's typing was even worse than usual. The misspellings and the deleted words jarred on him. They reminded him of what Peggy had said when she went off duty an hour ago. 'Jim's really looking ill. I don't think he should be here.' Peggy was not a person who exaggerated; nor was she prone to interfere in things that strictly weren't her business. And she had passed on a message from Dennis Lejeune, saying much the same thing in the guarded way that police doctors use. At present the Bureau could ill-afford to have anyone on sick leave.

Crozier picked up his phone and dialled Bergerac's home number.

'Susan? It's Barney Crozier. Can I have a word with Jim?'

'I wish you could. He's not back yet.'

'Where the hell is he?'

'How should I know?' Susan snapped. 'You do realize he shouldn't be working at all? He's not well.'

'That's what I wanted to talk about.' There was movement in the outer office. Crozier glanced through the open door. Bergerac had just come in. The room happened to be empty. He was swaying on his feet, for once making no attempt to conceal his exhaustion. 'Hold on, Susan. Talk of the devil. He's here.'

'Send him home, Barney. Please.'

'That's exactly what I'm going to do.'

At the sound of Crozier's voice, Bergerac straightened himself. Crozier put down the phone and beckoned him in.

'I don't want to see you again until Monday,' he said. 'And maybe not then. It depends on what the doctor says.'

Bergerac slumped into a chair. His face had the familiar obstinate expression that Crozier had come to loathe.

'Come off it, Barney. This case is just beginning to break. Dupont tied in the scarlet fever with that smuggling route I told you about. And Thornber's got a mistress in Carteret. She's almost certainly involved. Suppose Stroat had got wind of it? Dupont is going to talk to the woman tomorrow, and it would make sense if I went with him.'

'You're going to bed, Jim. You're not going to Carteret or anywhere else.'

'Look, Barney – '

'Shut up,' Crozier roared. Concern and irritation combined to feed his anger. Bergerac was running himself into the ground because he felt he was God's gift to criminal investigation; he couldn't believe that anyone could take his place.

Crozier made an effort and lowered his voice: 'We can cope quite well without you. You don't own the Stroat case.' Despite himself, the volume began to rise. 'And you're not the only detective we've got. You're a part of an organization. Dupont will keep us posted about the French end. I can switch Goddard away from the conference. At present you're not fit to hand out parking tickets. So go to bed and stay there. That's an order. And here's another order: you're not safe to drive in that condition. I'll get someone to take you home.'

Crozier reached for the internal phone and arranged for a squad car to pick up Bergerac at the main entrance.

Bergerac made no further attempt to argue. He sat, his face impassive, staring at the wall.

Crozier put down the phone. 'Susan's very worried, too.'

'I know.'

'You owe her something, Jim.'

'Yeah.' Bergerac stood up. 'I'll go and get my things. Good night.'

After Bergerac had left the office, Crozier sat motionless. He made no move to pick up the eighth report. His attempt to get through to Bergerac on a personal level had been an abject failure; Jim had never really got over the fact that he was now two rungs below Crozier on the promotion ladder, and likely to stay that way. Once they had been detective sergeants together: but that was a long time ago.

The doubts chased round his mind: maybe he should have handled Bergerac more gently; maybe he shouldn't have lost his temper; maybe he and Bergerac would always be like oil and water. It was true that no one in the Bureau was indispensable; but it was also true that Bergerac was the officer whom Crozier would find hardest to replace.

He opened the eighth report and yawned again. Man-management, he thought, was the hardest part of his job.

Last year they'd sent him on yet another course to learn how to do it. The course hadn't helped. Its organizers had never had to deal with a question that Crozier faced almost every day of his working life.

How the hell do you manage a man like Jim Bergerac?

Sergeant Corrance was on duty at the ground-floor reception. A sly smile flickered across his fat, white face as Bergerac came slowly down the stairs.

'Hullo, Jim,' he said. 'You look awful.'

Bergerac scowled at him. 'My taxi here yet?'

'Jeff Yardley's driving you. He phoned down to say he'd be five or ten minutes.'

'I'll go and have a leak.'

He continued down the stairs. In the basement he turned left, away from the cells, and walked purposefully down the corridor. He passed the lavatory without a second glance.

The records section was at the far end. He pushed open the door. An elderly constable was tidying the desk before handing over to the graveyard shift. He was a thin, gloomy man with a slight squint and an encyclopaedic knowledge of racing pigeons.

'You don't *want* anything, I hope?' He gestured at the cluttered desk. 'I was just . . .'

'Don't worry, Alf. Just wanted to check something. I can find it out myself.'

'Well, that's all right.' For the first time Alf saw Bergerac as a person, rather than as an irritating interruption. 'Are you OK? You look awful.'

'So they tell me.'

'Someone jumped you in the Odeon car park,' Alf told him; he was a man who enjoyed the circulation of information for its own sake, irrespective of any purpose it might or might not serve. 'If you ask me, you should be in bed. That Crozier's a slave driver.'

'Thanks for letting me know.'

Apart from the space near the door, where the desk was, the big, air-conditioned room was a network of steel shelving, some of it mounted on runners to maximize the use of the available space. The shelves were over six feet high. The introduction of computers at police headquarters had been heralded as the dawn of the paperless office. On the contrary, the computers generated even more paper than they had had before; and it still needed to be filed, stored and retrieved by hand.

Bergerac slipped into the labyrinth of shelving. He was almost immediately out of sight of Alf.

The constable's voice, as thin and gloomy as the man himself, droned on: 'Do us a favour, Jim – have a word with those youngsters of yours. What are they called? Pettit, that's one of them. Who's the other?'

'You mean Ben Lomas?' Bergerac ran his hand along one of the shelves. His fingers closed on a box-file.

'That's him. But it's the other one, really. That Pettit. Cheeky little bastard. They've got no respect, have they? They don't bother to look up the proper references for their reports – oh no, they leave that for me to do. And they come in here with their damn silly questions. It's "Alf, do this," and "Alf, where's that?" Who do they think they are? That's what I want to know. We weren't like that when we were young.'

The box-file was heavier than Bergerac expected; he almost dropped it. He leant against the shelves and leafed through its contents. He listened to Alf with half an ear, in case he needed to say something. Alf, he noted wryly, expected Bergerac to identify with him rather than with Lomas and Pettit.

'So will you do it, Jim?'

Bergerac realized that he had lost the thread of what Alf was saying. 'Do what?'

'Give them a bollocking. Teach them the facts of life. Just because they can call themselves detective constables, it doesn't mean they're God almighty. There's regulations. There's rules. And a few manners wouldn't do them any harm, either.'

'I'll have a word with them.' Bergerac found the mug shots. Full face and profile. A bruise on one cheek. The photographs had been taken just after the arrest. A strange, strong face, full of hate. The harsh lighting emphasized the bone structure. For an instant the face had a wholly unexpected familiarity: it reminded Bergerac of someone he had seen recently, but he couldn't remember who it was.

He was wasting time. If Yardley got impatient, he might phone Crozier; Crozier might come to look for him; and if he found him here, the balloon would go up.

Alf was describing in great detail some real or imagined sin that Willy Pettit had committed. Bergerac held the photographs in his mouth while he returned the box-file to its place. He glanced over his shoulder, making sure that Alf could not see him. He tucked the photographs in the inside pocket of his jacket.

It was strictly against the regulations. But Crozier had left him no option. All he had was a wild theory. They'd laugh at him if he mentioned it. All of them, from Crozier down to Willy Pettit.

And if anyone was going to test the theory, it had to be himself. This was his business and no one else's.

He emerged into the space around the desk. It seemed very hot down here. Alf had a cigarette in his mouth, and the tobacco smoke irritated Bergerac's throat. The wound in his side started to throb once more. There was a pain in his abdomen; maybe the attacker had found time to put the boot in last night. Last night seemed very long ago, but the thought of it made him feel slightly sick. The sweat gathered on his forehead. It cooled rapidly, presumably because of the air-conditioning, and he shivered.

Alf frowned at him. The cigarette drooped in the corner of his mouth. 'Are you all right?' he said again. 'You look as if you've seen a ghost.'

CHAPTER

11

'Will you be all right by yourself?' Susan asked.

She was wearing a charcoal grey suit with a faint pinstripe; she had her briefcase in one hand and the car keys in the other. She looked severe, professional and remarkably attractive.

'I'll be fine,' Bergerac said.

'Why are you smiling?'

The smile broadened into a grin. 'Because the roles are reversed, I suppose. Not that they were ever exactly traditional. Have a nice day at the office, dear.'

She ignored that. 'Are you sure you've got everything you'll need?'

Bergerac waved his hand round the room. 'What does it look like?'

He had the radio-cassette and the remote control for the television within easy reach. This morning's newspaper was on his lap. The breakfast tray and the telephone were on the bedside table. His dressing-gown, neatly folded, lay at the foot of the bed.

'I'll come back at lunchtime,' Susan said. 'You'll need something hot inside you.'

'I can do it myself,' Bergerac said quickly. 'I'm feeling much better this morning. I'll heat a tin of soup or something.'

'No, you won't.'

'But I don't want to mess up your day. You've got a living to earn. Someone's got to keep me in luxury.'

She bent down and kissed him. 'See you at one o'clock.'

He conceded defeat without a murmur. He had expected her to insist. In any case, if she didn't come she would phone instead, and that would be just as bad. In some ways phoning would have made it worse for her, because she would have had more scope for worry. It was a problem he couldn't solve. Facing consequences was part of the price he would have to pay. It occurred to him that Susan, too, would have to pay a share of the price.

The front door closed behind her. For ten minutes he nibbled toast and read the newspaper. It was best to leave a margin of safety in case Susan discovered that she had left something behind or remembered something else he might need. His conscience gave him a twinge but he refused to let it bother him. You couldn't please all of the people all of the time.

When he had finished the toast he reached for the phone and rang the Hotel de Bretagne.

'Henri? Could you pick me up at Susan's on your way to Gorey? I'm not going in to the Bureau this morning.'

'No problem, Jim.' Dupont sounded dazed.

'Enjoy yourself last night?'

There was a chuckle on the other end of the line. 'I'll see you in twenty minutes.'

Bergerac put down the phone and swung his legs out of bed. Yes, he decided, he was much better this morning, though his tongue felt rough. He swallowed two painkillers, just in case, and took his time over shaving and dressing. He scribbled a note – *Sorry, Sue – had to go out* – and left it on the bedside table. It was short to the point of being insulting; but it would have to do. There was really nothing he could say to make things better.

Dupont was prompt. There were bags under his eyes, and he didn't want to talk about his evening with Belle. They drove over to Gorey, returned the hire car and caught the vedette to Carteret. It was another fine day, and the sea was a clear, summer blue. The launch made the fifteen-mile crossing in under forty minutes. Neither of them said much during the journey. Bergerac tried to persuade himself that the fresh air was making him feel better. Once or twice he caught Henri watching him, with a thoughtful expression on his blunt features.

At the other end, Dupont's deputy was waiting for them in an unmarked Citroen. Michel shook hands with them both. He was a slight man with dark hair and a Marseilles accent. A white scar, an old knife wound, ran from his cheekbone to his chin. Bergerac had worked with him before.

'You haven't alarmed her, I hope?' Dupont said, once they were all in the car.

Michel started the engine. 'She knows nothing. I took the risk of not putting the café under surveillance. She's the kind of woman who can recognize a *flic* by instinct.'

'You've talked to the local men about her?'

'Nothing there. She keeps her nose clean. Her private life's her own concern – she's a widow, and she doesn't flaunt the boyfriends, so no one worries. I've seen her doctor, by the way. He says she's on her feet again, against his advice.'

The Café de la Libération was a whitewashed building overlooking the harbour. It was a modest place but well-maintained; and someone had recently added a glass-sided bar extension with a first-floor balcony on top.

Tables and chairs spilled out on to the forecourt. There were customers outside, enjoying the mid-morning sunshine. All of them were men, and most of them looked as if they made their living from the sea.

The three policemen threaded their way through the tables to the door of the bar. They attracted some suspicious glances from the clientele. One man, a squat sailor with tattoos on his arms, flicked the butt of his cigarette as they passed; it ricocheted off Bergerac's leg. This was not an establishment where unexpected visits by the police were welcomed.

Inside, the bar was very clean. It smelled of floor polish and freshly smoked Caporals. Machines with winking lights stood in a silent line against one wall, waiting for people to bring them to life by feeding them with money. Among them were pinball, table football, video games, fruit machines and an enormous jukebox.

At first, Bergerac thought the bar was empty. The extension was full of light but towards the back, in the older part of the room, there were many shadows. Someone stirred behind the counter.

Michel was already advancing into the bar. 'We wish to see Madame Proux.'

'*Madame est malade.*'

Bergerac's eyes adjusted to the relative gloom. He followed Michel and Henri towards the back of the room. The man behind the zinc-topped counter had 'bouncer' written all over him. He had a small head with squashed features; a massive chest was trying to escape from a T-shirt that had once been white. Beside his elbow on the counter was a glass of brandy.

'Police,' Michel said softly. He flashed his identification.

'You can't. The doctor says – '

'I've seen the doctor. She's well enough to see us.'

The door behind them opened. The squat sailor strolled into the bar. Outside, several of the other customers had changed chairs: now they were looking away from the harbour and into the bar.

Waiting for a signal . . .?

Bergerac calculated the odds: about two to one – better, if Michel was armed; worse, if he wasn't, because neither Bergerac nor Henri would be much use in a straight fight. But if Michel wasn't carrying, and those men were feeling reckless, the prospects were grim.

The barman straightened up to his full height. 'Madame

does not wish to see anyone. You must make an appointment.'

'Madame will see us.' Michel's voice was so low it was barely audible. He was standing on the balls of his feet.

No gun, Bergerac thought; *it's a lightweight jacket, and you'd see the bulge if he was wearing a holster.*

The barman lifted his glass and turned, as if he wanted to move it out of harm's way. The tattooed sailor raised his arm. The men outside stood up in a single, rippling movement, like a class before a teacher.

There was a moment's silence: the calm before the storm.

Then a woman's low-pitched voice said a single word: '*Non.*'

The tension evaporated. The barman took a sip from his glass. The sailor lowered his arm and pushed a coin into the pinball machine. The knot of men outside dissolved: some strolled away; others sat down again.

'Madame Proux?' It was the first time Henri had opened his mouth.

She was standing in a doorway to the right of the bar. Bergerac was conscious of a feeling of anticlimax. He had been expecting someone more flamboyant – a French version of Diamanté Lil, perhaps, with a sinister ingredient added to the formula; the Queen of Spades as opposed to the Queen of Diamonds.

'Come this way, *messieurs.*'

The first impression was one of dowdiness. *A black widow.* Madame Proux was a slight woman in her middle forties. Her dark hair was cut short and her black dress was anything but revealing. The three policemen followed her up a flight of stairs. She led them into a living room, linked by french windows to the balcony.

Dupont introduced his companions. She looked at them carefully but without emotion, like a farmer examining his neighbour's cattle at market.

Only then did Bergerac notice her eyes: they were large,

brown and astonishingly beautiful. Her skin was sallow, and the other features were plain; but the eyes and the intelligence behind them made the rest of her face irrelevant.

Madame Proux turned back to Dupont, as if realizing that he was the one that mattered. 'I apologize for François,' she said. 'He is overprotective. But that is what I pay him for, so the fault is mine. Would you like some coffee? Or a drink?'

He shook his head. 'You are quite recovered, Madame?'

She shrugged. 'Let us say I am better.'

'Scarlet fever is not a pleasant experience, I imagine. I am sorry that we have to trouble you.'

'It is nothing. Please sit down, if you wish.'

The room was large and furnished in complete contrast to the bar and its environs. It was a sanctuary of bourgeois values. The furniture was old and ugly; it was well-kept and would probably last for ever. There was china displayed on an ornate oak sideboard. Indifferent oil-paintings, expensively framed, hung on two of the walls. In one corner was an enormous flat-screen television, with a twin-deck VCR beneath.

Madame Proux sat, perfectly composed, waiting for their questions. Her hands lay on her lap. She wore a thin, gold wedding-band on her left hand, but no other jewellery.

Dupont cleared his throat. 'I believe you know a Monsieur Thornber? An Englishman with a boat called the *Golden Rialto*.'

She nodded almost imperceptibly.

'He stays here sometimes?'

Another nod.

'With you?' Dupont put a slight emphasis on the second word.

'That was correct.'

For the moment, Dupont ignored the implications of the tense she had used. 'Was he here at any time last week?'

'From the Monday to the Friday morning. He returned to Jersey on Friday but came back in the evening. He left again, in the early hours of Saturday morning.'

The voice was low-pitched and steady. She might have been reading aloud from a timetable.

'Do you know why he came to and from Carteret, Madame?'

The hands on her lap tightened, then relaxed. 'At first when he came I thought it was for me. Later, I began to think he had another motive as well. Last week, I realized that my presence or absence did not really concern him at all.'

'Then what was his real motive for coming here?'

'To this café? Because it is near the harbour. Because the police rarely come here. Because the customers do not gossip, and some of them will do most things for money. Because I was a sort of alibi for him: naturally a man must visit his mistress; so no one would dream that he had another reason for being here.'

The voice was still level, but now she was firing the sentences at Dupont like bursts from a machine-gun.

'I am sorry, Madame. We do not wish to cause you pain. But we must know what this reason was.'

'Sometimes . . .' She paused, twisting the wedding ring round and round her finger. 'Sometimes a customer would leave a package for him with me or François. Jack would take it away. I thought . . .'

'You thought he was smuggling.'

She frowned. 'Yes – but little things, you know. Everyone does that. It did not seem so very bad. But one of the men who brought a package got drunk. He didn't say much, but it was enough.'

'Cannabis?'

'That and other things, I think. Jack was using this place as a staging-post. The route goes south to Spain and Morocco. I do not know more about it than that.'

'Do you know what happened to it later? On Jersey?'

'How could I?' She spread her hands. 'He did not tell me much about his life there. I did not ask, either. I know he has a rich wife. He said once that he hated her, but perhaps that was a lie, too.'

Bergerac hardly dared to move. Michel stood like a statue by the window. Dupont was handling Madame Proux perfectly.

A question of his own, unwelcome and impossible to answer, surfaced in his mind: *Or is it the other way round? Is she handling him perfectly?*

Dupont was nodding. 'There must have been a straw,' he said slowly. 'The straw that broke the camel's back.'

'Last week, he did not smuggle something. He smuggled someone.'

'And who was that?'

'A woman. A woman whom Jack found attractive. That was your straw.'

'Ah.'

The monosyllable said it all. Half-grunt, half-sigh, it expressed Dupont's admiration for Madame Proux; it condemned the treacherous folly of Jack Thornber; it suggested that Dupont found Thornber's preference for another woman completely inexplicable.

'He brought the woman here?'

'She stayed in one of the rooms upstairs. She arrived on Tuesday. She was to leave that night, but she was too ill. They had to wait until she was better. It was she who brought the scarlet fever here. Jack was angry at first, but she won him over. I think that Jack had to go back to Jersey on Friday to make new arrangements.'

'Did you learn her name?'

Madame Proux shook her head. 'She is a big woman in her thirties. The hair was short and dark, but I think it was dyed. They talked in English together, very fast.'

'You understand English, Madame?'

'A little. Enough for my customers.'

'You tried to listen to their conversation, naturally,' Dupont suggested, 'as any reasonable person would have done.'

'Naturally,' she agreed. 'But they were careful. One thing I heard was this, as Jack was leaving the woman's room. I was on the stairs and he did not see me. He said, "*Prie-nasse* is there," and the woman replied, "On Jersey?" Then he saw me standing there.'

'*Prie-nasse*,' Dupont repeated. Like Madame Proux he pronounced it as though it were two French words. Literally they meant 'pray' and 'rat trap'. He glanced at Bergerac and then back to the woman. 'A name, you think?'

She shrugged. 'Possibly. How should I know?'

Dupont leant forward. 'Did either of them leave anything here? Anything at all? Clothes, for example, or money?'

She stood up. 'The woman left nothing. I have even had the floorboards up in the room she used. I have put everything that belongs to Jack in the suitcase. In here.'

Dupont followed her out of the room. She opened a deep cupboard on the landing and indicated a battered leather suitcase. Dupont pulled it out, and they returned to the living room.

He gestured from the case to the floor. 'You permit, Madame?'

She shrugged again.

The case was unlocked. Dupont threw back the lid. Bergerac leant over the arm of his chair to get a better view. Inside was a jumble of clothes, a pile of dog-eared sailing magazines, tied together with string, a toothbrush and a faded blue face-flannel. Everything looked and smelled slightly damp; perhaps the flannel had not been dry when Madame Proux tossed it on top of the clothes.

Dupont took his time with the contents. He examined every item, paying particular attention to those that had pockets. The yield was disappointing: a few centimes, a crumpled paper handkerchief, a good deal of fluff and, pushed into the change pocket of a pair of jeans, a scrap of white paper. He unfolded the paper and smoothed it out. Then he passed it to Bergerac.

It was a receipt, torn from the roll of an electronic till. Delanier et Cie had accepted the sum of 540 francs from a customer. The date was last Thursday's.

Dupont nodded towards Madame Proux. Bergerac handed the receipt to her.

She put on a pair of glasses and looked at it, frowning. 'It means nothing to me. Jack borrowed the car on Thursday morning. He said he wanted some supplies for the boat.'

Dupont refastened the suitcase. 'You have been very helpful, Madame. I think we need trouble you no more for the present. Unless, of course, there is something you wish to add?'

She returned the glasses to their case. 'There is nothing, Monsieur. Nothing except . . .'

'Except what?'

'I hope you get him. And when you do, tell him that I helped you.' Her voice was so cool that she might have been discussing an unpaid bill; perhaps in a way she was. 'If he ever comes here again, I shall see that he suffers.'

'Monsieur Thornber is not a wise man.' Dupont struggled to his feet and held out his hand. 'And now – '

'Henri?' Bergerac said. 'May I ask a question?'

Dupont nodded, but Bergerac could tell that he was not enthusiastic about the request. That was natural. Like the good interrogator he was, Henri had devoted much effort to building up a one-to-one relationship with Madame Proux. The blundering intervention of an outsider could upset the delicate understanding between them.

Bergerac stood up. The wound in his side protested at the change in position, and for an instant he thought his legs were too weak to bear his weight. The moment passed. He pulled from his pocket the mugshots he had removed from the records section last night. Without a word, he handed them to Madame Proux.

Once more she put on her glasses. She stared at the photographs. Her eyelids dropped over her eyes, giving her a sudden resemblance to a bird of prey.

'Her face is thinner now,' she said to Dupont. 'And she's cut her hair and dyed it. But there's no doubt about it: that's the bitch who came here.'

CHAPTER
12

The anxiety rapidly turned to anger.

He hadn't even bothered to wash up his breakfast things.

Then she found the note on the bedside table. *Sorry, Sue – had to go out.* Her control snapped, and she threw the fillet of plaice on the floor. She ground it into the carpet. The heel of her shoe split the paper and fragments of moist, white fish oozed out.

He must have been planning this all along. No doubt he had the usual stupid justification in what he was pleased to call his mind: duty called, so to hell with her feelings and his own state of health. Except this time it wasn't even duty, because Barney Crozier had ordered him to take sick leave. No, he was obeying the dictates of his private and highly selective moral code. In other words, Jim Bergerac was playing God again.

Well, she'd had enough. In future he could make his own toast and fetch the thermometer himself.

The decision made, she felt calmer. The clothes he'd been wearing yesterday were gone. But the car was still outside; he'd retained enough sense not to drive. So what was he doing? Ten to one it was connected with the Stroat murder. It couldn't be official, because the Bureau knew he was on sick leave. Who else was tied up with it? Belle, maybe – or Henri Dupont. But Dupont was meant to be at the conference.

She picked up the phone and dialled the Bureau.

Peggy answered the call. By the sound of it she was halfway through a sandwich.

'You've not seen Jim, have you?' Susan asked.

'No, of course not. He's meant to be off sick until Monday.'

'Can you get in touch with Barney?'

'I could in theory,' Peggy said hesitantly. 'But only if it's vital. He's at the Bretagne, you see – it's the last day of the conference. But he's not very – '

'This *is* vital,' Susan interrupted. 'Jim's swanned off to do a bit of private sleuthing, and I think Barney should know.'

'Oh, dear. The Chief Inspector won't be very happy about that.'

'I realize that,' Susan said with some satisfaction. 'But he ought to be told. Jim's not safe to be out on his own.'

'All right. I'll get on to him.'

Susan put the phone down. She had trodden on the fish again, this time by accident.

It was all such a mess.

'A vengeful woman,' Henri said, 'is a force to be reckoned with.' Without warning, he swung the Citroen's wheel to the left, pulled out and overtook a Mercedes; he was an adventurous but appalling driver. 'A woman scorned,' he went on placidly, 'is a fury, an elemental power, a – '

'You nearly hit that lorry,' Bergerac said. 'Do you think you could watch the road?'

Instead, Dupont glanced at his passenger. 'You are not yourself. In the café, I thought you were going to faint at one point.'

'I'm OK. Just a bit shaky.' Bergerac shifted his aching body in the seat and shifted the conversation away from his health. 'So you think Madame Proux was on the level?'

'Without a doubt. I know that type of woman.' Dupont nodded rather smugly, hinting that, like so many French-men, he was an authority on the subject of the other sex.

'But tell me – why didn't you contact Chief Inspector Crozier before we left Carteret?'

'I'd rather check out this lead first.'

'But surely the matter is urgent? And whatever we learn now, it is unlikely to change that.'

By now they had reached the outskirts of Caen. The sky had clouded over since the morning, and the old city looked grey and unwelcoming. Only the two of them were in the car; Michel had stayed in Carteret. Dupont turned north, away from the old town, and followed a zigzag course through a series of side roads.

'You play your cards very close to your chest, Jim,' he said as he changed down for another corner. 'That can be a weakness. I don't think Crozier knows you're here.'

They travelled another hundred yards before Bergerac replied.

'Technically I'm on sick leave. Barney's a stickler for the rules.'

'Your rules don't concern me. But Thornber does. If this delay means we lose him . . .'

'We won't. He's not going anywhere. He's ill.'

Dupont grunted. 'You're ill, too. Yet here you are.'

They turned into a broad avenue, lined with high-rise flats, light-industrial premises and small shops. Dupont swore, made a U-turn that nearly led to an argument with an articulated lorry and pulled over to the pavement on the other side of the road.

They were beside a shabby shop. The sign above the window said DELANIER ET CIE. In the window was a chaise longue, upholstered in yellow velvet. On it reclined a tailor's dummy, dressed in what looked like an eighteenth-century gown. At the head of the chaise was a stand that supported a stuffed parrot in an advanced stage of decomposition.

'Appearances are deceptive,' Dupont said as they got out

of the car. 'According to Michel, you'd have to go to Paris to match what Delanier has to offer.'

'You wouldn't think there'd be the demand.'

'You're wrong. Who in their right mind would buy a costume or a prop if they can rent it? Film companies on location. Provincial theatres. Amateur dramatic societies.'

The interior was much larger than the shopfront suggested. It was crammed with a bizarre collection of objects, most of them large and garish. The range was catholic: you could get anything from a fake Jacobean sideboard to a weather-stained statue of Neptune. A hand-lettered sign directed them to the costume department at the rear of the building.

It seemed to Bergerac that they had to walk for miles. Eventually they reached a single-storey annex at the back. It had a corrugated-iron roof, a concrete floor and windows which were opaque with grime. It looked as if it had been erected as temporary industrial accommodation in about 1943. Dusty strip-lights hummed above their heads. Racks of costumes, each shrouded with a transparent plastic cover, filled most of the floor space. There was a strong smell of dry-cleaning fluid.

An elderly man shuffled out of a tiny office that had been created by partitioning off a corner of the annexe.

'*Messieurs?*' he mumbled.

'Police,' Dupont said curtly. As a policeman, he treated women with consideration, but he was inclined to bully the men as a matter of course. The attendant shrank away as Dupont advanced towards him. 'We wish to trace this transaction.'

The man took the receipt. A drop of moisture trembled on the end of his nose.

'It is impossible,' he said. 'We have no means of knowing without a full receipt.'

'It was an Englishman,' Bergerac said. 'He had a red beard, and he probably paid cash.'

'Ah! I served him myself.' The old man grinned unexpectedly, revealing red, swollen gums and three crooked teeth; the movement dislodged the drop of moisture. 'The Englishman who was in a hurry. The Englishman who wanted to dress up as a nun.'

Thornber was in a hurry.

The scarlet fever had given him five days of agony – not just because of the illness, but because it gave him time to think while making it impossible for him to act.

He had no means of making contact himself, so he had yearned for this phone call. He had also dreaded it, because of the possibility that someone else would reach the phone before him. In the event, however, the timing couldn't have been better. Mary was down at the Orchid Factory. The cleaning woman didn't come in on Thursdays. He himself was already out of bed and trying to dress himself. He had promised Mary that he would sit on the sofa in the drawing room and watch television.

The familiar voice proposed a time and place. Thornber agreed at once, despite the risk. Any action was better than none.

Physically, he felt better; but the worry was almost killing him. He had followed the case in the papers and on the radio. According to the media, the police were getting nowhere, but that was too good to be true. After all, they had already sniffed him out. In his heart of hearts he knew they were waiting to pounce.

Hurry. His fingers fumbled with the buttons of his shirt. It was as though they had to learn the technique all over again. That damned scarlet fever had drained the strength and skill from his muscles. He was already a couple of minutes late.

While he struggled into his clothes, the familiar thoughts blundered through his mind. He had been a fool to get involved in the first place. It should have been such a straightforward, lucrative job – and potentially pleasant, too, for the woman had bedroom eyes. Now he knew better. She didn't get her kicks from sex. That terrible scene on the beach seemed to have taken root in his mind. When the fever was at its height, he had lived through it again and again.

The only sensible course was to keep his options open. There was no immediate risk: she needed him more than he needed her. He would wait to hear what the meeting produced. If it wasn't enough to convince him that he was safe, maybe he should cut his losses and turn Queen's Evidence. It wouldn't be pleasant but the alternative would be far worse.

He walked slowly downstairs, clutching the handrail for support. The house was very quiet. *Hurry.* In the hall he shrugged on his jacket and wrapped a scarf carefully round his neck. He had to look after himself; he was still convalescent.

Though the sky had clouded over since the early morning, the light outside made him blink. There was a pair of sunglasses in his pocket. He put them on and walked slowly down the drive. It felt good to be outside. He hated being confined. What he really needed was to be aboard the *Golden Rialto*, with a stiff sea breeze blowing away the sickroom smells and the remnants of infection. Of course that was out of the question: at present he was far too weak to handle the boat single-handed.

Before the drive reached the belt of firs, he veered away to the right. It would never do to allow Mary to see him. Her office window overlooked the drive as it came through the trees. He followed the line of the plantation towards the road. *Hurry, hurry.* Mary kept this part of the garden as a contrived wilderness. The grass was long, and studded with bluebells. Even through the glasses, the colours were uncomfortably vivid.

A low whistle on his left made him turn his head.

At first he could see nothing. Beneath the branches of the firs, the plantation was reduced to a thick green shadow. Thornber took off the sunglasses.

A figure in black was standing among the trees. He raised a hand in greeting. The figure moved forward, beckoning him.

The sun chose that moment to burst through a gap in the clouds. It glinted on something metallic at the end of a long, black sleeve.

Thornber stopped. It was hard to breathe. He was trapped in the sunlight like a fly in amber. The glasses slipped unheeded from his hand. His head was about to burst.

Then, at last, he understood. *Hurry.*

He swung round, almost losing his balance in the process, and tried to force his legs to run.

CHAPTER
13

Crozier slammed down the phone. Breathing heavily, he forced himself to count to ten. Then he slipped back to the hall.

It was already filling up for the afternoon session. The atmosphere was markedly livelier than it had been in the morning. The conference was nearly over, and the relief of many of the delegates, helped in many cases by the intake of alcohol at lunch, had created an air of festivity. Prinknash had his hands in his pockets and a smile on his face; he was standing in the central gangway, talking to one of the organizers. As Crozier watched, he threw back his head and laughed.

Not a care in the world.

Crozier beckoned Goddard, who was positioned between Prinknash and the door. 'I've got to go back to the Bureau,' he said. 'You and Willy are going to have to manage Prinknash by yourselves.'

'Trouble?' Goddard said.

Crozier turned away without answering. Before Peggy phoned, his temper had already been simmering. It had already been a rough day, what with the appalling tedium of the conference, Prinknash's misplaced heroism, the paperwork mounting up back at the office and press criticisms about the Bureau's handling of the Stroat case. But now his rage was about to boil over. He didn't want to waste any on Goddard if he could help it.

In the corridor outside the conference hall, he bumped – literally – into Charlie Hungerford.

'Lost your glasses, Barney?' Hungerford waved his cigar in Crozier's face, scattering ash over the carpet. 'And where are you off to? The session's about to begin.'

'I've got to get back to the Bureau.'

'But you'll miss my keynote speech.'

'Sorry. I can't help that.'

Crozier's tone suggested that he didn't regret it, either. Hungerford bristled automatically at the insult. But when he opened his mouth, curiosity had outweighed damaged pride.

'What's the rush?' he said. 'A new development? You're on the verge of an arrest?'

'It's a disciplinary matter,' Crozier said, trying to edge past Hungerford. 'Urgent but internal.'

'Then can't it wait?' Hungerford leant casually against the wall, blocking Crozier's manoeuvre. 'If something happens to Sir Vernon, you'll be held responsible, you know.'

'I wish something *would* happen to him,' Crozier muttered.

'What was that?'

'I said nothing will happen to him, not with Goddard and Pettit here. Besides, you know as well as I do that Prinknash would probably enjoy it if something *did* happen. Give him a chance to hit the Nine O'Clock News.'

'He wouldn't enjoy it if he's dead.'

'Prinknash seems prepared to take that risk.'

'Did I hear my name?'

Crozier swung round. Sir Vernon was strolling up the corridor from the conference hall, with Goddard and Pettit hovering anxiously beside him. If the threat of his impending demise had put him under any strain, his face wasn't showing it.

'I was just explaining to Mr Hungerford that I have to go back to the Bureau,' Crozier said. 'I'll be back later.'

'You've had some news about my contract killer?' Prinknash sounded as though he had a possessive, almost paternal interest in the man.

'It's nothing to do with that, sir. I wish it were.'

'"A disciplinary matter," I gather,' Hungerford said scornfully. '"Urgent but internal." Personally, I would have thought that saving a man's life was rather more urgent than giving some underling a rap over the knuckles, but that's neither here nor there.' He sniffed. 'I'm not a trained professional like the Chief Inspector.'

Pettit had a smirk on his face. Crozier made a mental note of it.

'I'm sure the Chief Inspector has excellent reasons for whatever he does,' Prinknash said smoothly. He smiled at Crozier. 'It all comes down to manpower in the end, doesn't it? If you could double the Bureau's establishment, this sort of problem wouldn't arise.'

'Yes. I'm sorry, sir: I must go.'

Crozier made his escape. He hurried through the hotel's reception, down the steps and into the car park.

Urgent but internal – that was exactly right. In their different ways, both guarding Prinknash and attending the conference were important. But other people could guard Prinknash; and the conference would survive without one of the many middle-ranking policemen in the audience.

But the Bureau was different. The Bureau was Crozier's responsibility, and so were the men under him. He couldn't run the place without discipline. One of his subordinates had flagrantly disobeyed his orders: that was the sin against the Holy Ghost.

When he reached the car, the radio was trying to attract his attention.

'Chief Inspector?' It was Detective Constable Wilson. 'I have Detective Sergeant Bergerac on the phone for you. Shall I patch him through?'

'Yes,' Crozier snarled. 'Where's he calling from?'

'Caen, sir.'

'What the hell's he doing there? Sightseeing? No, don't answer, you fool. Put him through to me.'

Crozier registered the fact that Wilson was using all the formalities of rank. The DC was playing for safety. That meant the news of Bergerac's latest escapade had filtered through the Bureau's grapevine. The rank and file were running for cover before the explosion.

'Barney – '

'Sergeant Bergerac! I want you back on this island. As soon as a doctor certifies you fit, you'll be up before a board of – '

'Shut up, will you?'

'*What* did you say?'

'I'll face the firing squad, whatever you want.' Bergerac's voice had an almost hysterical edge that Crozier had never heard before. 'But first, is there a nun at that conference?'

'Have you gone off your rocker, Bergerac?'

'Get back inside the hotel and check. And pull Thornber in; Dupont wants to collar him for smuggling, and we may have other charges.'

The stream of orders infuriated Crozier. But he said calmly, 'What's this about a nun?'

'The person gunning for Prinknash is probably disguised as a nun. It isn't a he, it's a she. For God's sake, hurry, Barney: it's Norma Jean Veldman.'

Mary Thornber began to worry after the first time she failed to get through.

But she was a sensible woman, who took pride in the fact that she rarely panicked. Maybe Jack had gone to the lavatory. Maybe he was having a bath. Maybe he was asleep. She returned resolutely to the third and final draft of the Orchid Factory's Summer Catalogue.

The *Paphiopedilum* section covered the slipper orchids. They were doing well, though of course May was the time of year when they were at their best. Still, the sales figures meant that the unit costs had dropped rather more than she had expected. They should be able to lower prices by five per cent for the next three months – the boom period for tourist visitors – and still make a profit, even if sales did not maintain the spring rate of growth. But with luck, lower prices would generate more sales.

She keyed the revised figures into the computer and checked the results against the projected sales for the next six months. It would definitely work. She turned back to the word-processor and substituted the new prices for the old. The big question now was whether she could manage to do the same for the moth orchids.

But the *Phalaenopsis* section failed to hold her attention. Perhaps it wasn't such a big question after all. Not at present. Mary Thornber sighed. She wasn't panicking, she told herself, but she was sensible enough to know that personal worries got in the way of work. She picked up the phone and called the house again.

The phone rang on and on. No one answered.

'Jackie?'

Mrs Le Vare looked up.

'I'm just going over to the house for a few minutes. If Canton's arrive with the fertilizer, tell the man to wait. I wasn't satisfied with the last lot. I want to see it before we accept delivery.'

Mrs Thornber walked up the drive. The trim grounds and the neat buildings soothed her. They were a tangible sign of the order and financial security that she had imposed on chaos and near-bankruptcy, after the collapse of Jack's chandlery business on the mainland. She had done it herself. She had saved them both.

The front door was locked. That came as no surprise, for Mrs Thornber had strong views on security, and she had long ago persuaded Jack to accept them. Jersey might be more law-abiding than the mainland but there were still plenty of criminals, attracted to the smell of money like wasps to a jam-pot.

'It's me, Jack,' she called as she opened the door. She could see at once that he wasn't on the sofa in the drawing room.

There was no reply. She went quickly upstairs and into his room. The bed was unmade and he wasn't there, but the room still smelled of his presence. It was a strange moment for her to remember that they had not slept together for some time – they stopped sharing a bed around the time when the chandlery business plunged irretrievably into the red. Jack's snoring had always disturbed her.

He was not in the en-suite bathroom, either. She checked the rest of the house with swift efficiency. Then she returned to his room. *A territorial odour that somehow excludes me . . .* The components included aftershave, the cigarettes he wasn't supposed to smoke, leather and an indefinable tang that reminded her of the sea.

The pyjamas were on the bed: so he was up and dressed. Suddenly and shamefully, she was on the verge of panic. Her secret fear was out in the open: *Jack has left me.* She almost ran to the dressing-table.

To her relief, the car keys and his wallet were still there, along with the cheque book and the driving licence. He had taken nothing but the house keys. She wiped the sweat from her forehead with a paper handkerchief. The fear receded.

It was quite simple, she told herself. The sun had come out, and Jack hadn't been able to resist going outside. He hated being cooped up. And after nearly a week in bed, the desire for fresh air must have been overwhelming. But he should have had the sense to phone the office and let her know.

But he wouldn't do that, would he? Because I'd have told him that he wasn't to exert himself. I'd have kept him indoors and made him take things easy on the sofa.

126

She pushed the thought away. He was somewhere in the garden: she would find him in a moment or two. That was what mattered. And when she found him, he was going to regret his irresponsibility.

A car was coming up the drive. The belt of firs acted as a sound barrier. You could always tell if a car was coming to the house, rather than to the Orchid Factory, because the engine noise would suddenly increase in volume once the car was past the trees. She went to the window.

A car skirted the fountain and pulled up at the bottom of the flight of steps that led to the front door. From her vantage point, she noticed that the gleaming paintwork of its roof was marred by a curving smear of white; it was a bird-dropping in motion. The stain stood out with a clarity that was almost painful. As soon as the car stopped, four men got out, two of them in uniform.

The police?

Panic bubbled inside her. The fear was out in the open and she would never be able to force it back into hiding.

An accident? Jack, my love, why did you leave me?

The nun unlocked the cupboard in the bedroom.

The cupboard had originally been designed as a wardrobe. It filled an alcove by the fireplace from floor to ceiling. At the top was a long, metal rail to hold the hangers. But at present there were no clothes inside, apart from the shirt and trousers that the man was wearing.

His wrists were lashed together with wire. They were tied above the rail, and she had knotted the wire tightly to the rail itself, so the man could not slide his wrists from side to side. The space permitted him to stand, albeit with his neck on one side, his legs bent and his shoulders hunched. He couldn't sit; he couldn't lean against the wall; he couldn't lower his arms. Any movement he made tended to tighten the wire round his wrists.

She had removed his shoes before she went out, in case

he tried to attract attention by kicking the cupboard door. No one would have heard him but she hoped the measure would have a psychological effect.

His eyes were open. She was pleased to see that he had been crying. The tears had zigzagged through the dirt on his cheeks. Perhaps cramp was responsible for them, but with luck it might be fear. She wanted him to be afraid with a passion that surprised even her.

The gag bisected his face. She undid the scarf and pulled out the rag it held in place.

He retched weakly.

'Well?' she said.

'Water.' The word was barely distinguishable from a groan. 'Please.'

'We've been through all this before,' she said irritably. 'Not until you cooperate. Then you can have all the water you bloody well want. You can drown in the stuff for all I care. Lovely, cool, *wet* water.'

She left him for a moment and went to the kitchen. She filled a glass from the tap and returned to the bedroom. In this job it often paid to use your head rather than your muscles; and in many ways it could be much more amusing.

He couldn't keep his eyes off the glass in her hand; that was all to the good. She drank the water slowly, watching his face. Twice she held the glass towards him. Once she touched his lips with the rim, jerking it away when he bent forward. When there was only half an inch left, she poured the water down the side of his face and watched his dry, swollen tongue trying and failing to catch a drop of moisture.

But he said nothing. *The obstinate old bastard.*

'Look,' she said, fumbling in her pocket.

It was a large clasp-knife with a blade that locked in place. She had bought it in a shop that catered for fishermen. She opened it and showed him the blade with the dull, rusting stain. In a while she would boil the stain away in the kitchen, but there was no harm in trying out its potential as a visual aid.

'It's all your fault, you know,' she said conversationally. 'You could stop all this in a moment if you'd only be reasonable. Do you think I enjoy this?'

He was nodding! The bastard was nodding! She hit him twice across the face with her free hand. He of all people had no right to sit in judgement over her.

'Right,' she snapped. 'If you want me to get rough, I shall.' She retied the gag, jerking his head violently from side to side. 'This is just the beginning, you know. The gentle art of persuasion. But tonight I'll try something else.'

His eyes stared into hers. It struck her that they were neither angry nor afraid: they were sad.

'Once I really get going, it's not a question of *if* you'll crack. Just *when*. And believe me, it won't be long. Once I get serious, it never takes long.'

She slammed the cupboard door and turned the key in the lock. When she tried to light a cigarette, her hand was shaking so much that she dropped the first match. The mentholated smoke made her cough; her throat was still sore. She threw the cigarette into the empty fireplace.

It would have been so much easier if he had been angry or scared. Anything but that patronizing sorrow. He had always been like that; she had never been able to arouse anger or fear in him.

My one and only failure?

But she didn't believe in eternal verities like 'always' and 'never'. Maybe she could never teach him to be angry. But by God she could teach him the meaning of fear.

CHAPTER
14

When the French decided to cooperate, there was nothing mean about them. They cooperated as they cooked: in style.

The helicopter descended into the field near Government House. Bergerac watched the grass flattening beneath them. He was the only passenger. Dupont would be back in Carteret by now, asking delicate questions at the Café de la Libération while his men tore the place apart, probably with sledgehammers.

The racket of the rotors, even though muted by the ear-muffs, went through Bergerac's head like a pneumatic drill. Usually he was a good traveller, but the flight had made him queasy, despite the lack of turbulence. Since they had reached the Channel, he had been fighting back the urge to be sick. He longed to be on land again.

A police car was waiting on the access road. As he watched, the driver's door opened and Goddard got out. That was something. Bergerac had been half-afraid that Crozier would turn up in person, along with his favourite set of handcuffs.

The helicopter touched down with a jolt. Bergerac unbuckled himself and nodded his thanks to the police pilot, who would be flying straight back to his base at Caen. He swung the hatch open and jumped down to the ground. The drop was shorter than he had anticipated. He stumbled and almost fell over. The blades of grass rippled beneath him, as though the earth itself was gently vibrating.

He lowered his head, hunched his shoulders and jogged

towards the access road. The down-draught from the rotors felt like a giant's hand, gently pressing him towards the earth.

Goddard already had the engine running. The car, a Granada, began to move before Bergerac had time to close the door. They skirted the grounds of Government House and came out on St Saviour's Hill.

'You've nicked Thornber?'

Goddard shook his head. 'He went missing, sometime between eleven and half-past two. And there's no sign of Norma Jean, either.'

As they drove down the hill to St Helier, he briefed Bergerac on what had happened since Bergerac had talked to Crozier from Caen.

'Leave's been cancelled throughout the force. Crozier's down at the Bretagne with his private task-force. It's not just the Bureau – we've got teams from Operations and Crime, too. They're taking the hotel apart. Some of the delegates are furious, and the press are jumping up and down. We'll be getting complaints about police brutality and infringing the rights of the individual if we don't watch out.'

They had reached Rouge Bouillon. Bergerac swallowed. The nausea seemed to be worse, not better, since he had landed.

Goddard glanced at him. 'I hope you're right about Veldman. If you're not, there'll be hell to pay.'

'I got a positive ID in Carteret,' Bergerac said. 'From Thornber's mistress.'

'Let's hope it holds up.'

'What are we doing about Thornber? The French are going to hate it if we lose him.'

'The usual. An all-island alert. Local radio and TV flashes. We're going to have the dogs out at the Orchid Factory.'

'You've checked Thornber's boat?'

'Leave it out.' Goddard stopped for a traffic light. His voice had hardened. 'We're not totally incompetent without you to tell us what to do. The *Golden Rialto*'s at its moorings. His car's in the garage.' He let out the clutch. 'Thornber seems to have taken nothing with him, not even his wallet. His passport's still at the house.'

'So he's with someone?'

'Either that or he's communing with nature.'

'There's one other possibility,' Bergerac said.

'We all know that.' Goddard signalled left and turned into police headquarters. 'Crozier wants you to get over to St Brelade and coordinate the search.'

'Then what are we doing here?'

'I've got to pick up some mug shots of Veldman and Thornber. You want to wait in the car?'

Bergerac came into the building with Goddard. He reached the lavatory just in time. As soon as he opened his mouth, he lost his lunch. Maybe it was something he had eaten, or even delayed shock. He felt better for vomiting, and better still after he had rinsed his mouth and washed his hands. His face in the mirror looked like a stranger's: the bandage, now slightly askew, elongated his skull; and his skin was red and puffy.

He ought to phone Susan. But there wasn't time. In any case, what had he got to say? He had a strong suspicion that 'sorry' wouldn't cut much ice with her, any more than it would with Barney Crozier. Besides, he didn't really regret what he had done. All he regretted was hurting Susan. Crozier was another matter: he wasn't hurt, just furious.

It was something that Barney was treating him as on-duty. But that was just a temporary relief, for the duration of this alert. Crozier would neither forget nor forgive Bergerac's disobedience.

When he got back to the car, Goddard was already there; he was drumming his fingers on the steering wheel.

He frowned. 'Are you OK, Jim?'

'Fine,' Bergerac said. 'Never better.'

The Granada moved smoothly out of the parking slot. Neither of them talked during the journey along the coast and up to St Brelade. The latest dose of painkillers was beginning to wear off. Luckily Bergerac had the bottle in his pocket.

At the Orchid Factory, the dog-handlers' van was parked in the drive. Goddard drove on to the house. The dogs were following the line of the belt of firs, heading towards the road. They were tugging against the handlers' leads. Lomas and two uniformed officers brought up the rear. Lomas, hearing the car's engine, turned and gave them a thumbs-up sign.

'He looks so bloody happy,' Bergerac said.

Goddard shrugged. 'Ten or twelve years ago, he was probably playing cops-and-robbers. This job's not so very different, sometimes. Looks like they've got a scent.'

'Where's Mrs Thornber?' Bergerac asked suddenly.

'In the house. No more questions, the doc said, not for a while. There's a WPC with her.'

The dogs vanished into the trees. The men went with them. Bergerac and Goddard waited. A moment later, Lomas reappeared. He plodded slowly towards the car. His shoulders were bent, as though he were carrying an invisible rucksack. His face was very pale. No one would have accused him of looking happy now.

There was a lot of blood.

It had soaked into the ground around the body, dyeing the carpet of pine needles. The light was poor because the body was surrounded by trees. The dogs were back in their van. One of them was whining softly.

A scene-of-the-crime team was on its way. Fortunately Lejeune was already on the spot; it was he who had seen

Mrs Thornber. He knelt beside the body, absorbed in his work.

Thornber's face was no longer ruddy. His beard was the colour of a fox's fur. He lay on his back with his limbs outstretched. The eyes and the mouth were open. Some people found an unexpected dignity in death; Thornber was not among them.

'No sign of the knife,' Goddard said. 'Maybe it's under the body.'

'I doubt it,' Dr Lejeune said. He folded back the collar of Goddard's coat and shone his torch on the neck. 'But of course you never know. I don't want to move him yet.'

Bergerac was leaning against the trunk of a tree. 'Not a suicide?' The words came out as a croak. It hurt him to speak.

'I prefer not to be categorical at this stage.'

'I don't want you to be categorical.' The pain made him curt. 'I want an opinion.'

Lejeune glanced up at him. 'You shouldn't be here at all, Jim. Anyway, all I'm really sure about is that he's dead.'

'Come off it, Dennis. I haven't got all day.' As soon as the words were out, Bergerac regretted that he had shown his irritation. Antagonizing Lejeune was pointless.

The doctor sat back on his haunches. 'All right,' he said coldly. 'Quite apart from the absence of the knife, it doesn't look like this wound was self-inflicted. Suicidal throat-cutting generally looks clean and deliberate. This is a jagged cut, deeper in some places than in others. So maybe Thornber was struggling. There again, suicides usually arch their necks – like that.' He demonstrated with his own neck, a few feet away from Thornber's. 'That makes the carotid arteries slip back. As a result the knife often misses them, so the blood loss is reduced.' He gestured at the ground. 'Which obviously wasn't the case here.'

'So you think it was murder?'

Lejeune's shoulders twitched with irritation. 'Let's say

that the probabilities point in that direction. At present.'
His mouth set in an obstinate line. 'Can't be definite until
I've done the PM.'

'Time of death?'

'Don't be ridiculous. I'm not a clairvoyant.'

'Could a woman have done it?'

'Possibly.' Lejeune spread his hands, inviting sympathy
from the other men that stood in a silent circle round the
body. 'It's a pity I forgot to pack my crystal ball.'

Someone smothered a laugh. Bergerac couldn't be bothered to find out who it was. He waited patiently, conserving
his energy. After a few seconds, the doctor's good nature
reasserted itself.

'Thornber wasn't a weakling, like Stroat was,' he said
slowly. 'But the scarlet fever must have left him feeling like
a wet rag. A woman could have done it – if she was strong
and if she was lucky or knew what she was doing. Or if she
hated him enough – it's surprising what you can do if
you're really angry. And of course she might have taken
him by surprise. But don't you dare quote me.'

'Can you tell if the attacker came – '

'Sarge,' Lomas said urgently. 'Someone's coming.'

Bergerac looked round. The grass muffled the sound of
running feet. Mary Thornber was sprinting across the lawn;
her dressing-gown flew behind her like a pair of wings. The
WPC was on the steps from the front door, gamely giving
chase but too far away to have a hope of catching her
charge.

Goddard said softly, 'Oh, bloody *hell*!'

'Stop her!' Bergerac snapped.

They were too late. Mrs Thornber burst into the belt of
trees and blundered into the circle of policemen. Her face
was white with a tinge of grey, the colour of newspaper,
and the muscles around her mouth were working strangely.
By contrast, her cropped grey hair was as well-groomed as
though she had just come out of a hairdresser's.

Goddard tried to grab her but she evaded his arm, probably accidentally, by dropping to her knees. She was only a few inches away from Jack Thornber's feet. Her chest was heaving. She stared at the body but made no attempt to touch him.

'How dare you?' she screamed. 'How *dare* you leave me?'

'We'll be leaving now, Mr Jollyon,' Crozier said. 'Thank you again for your cooperation.'

The assistant manager dabbed his lips with a handkerchief. 'Chief Inspector, have you any idea of the effect this . . . this *charade* is going to have on our bookings?'

'I'm sorry, sir. I'm sure you appreciate – '

'You've turned the whole hotel upside down,' Jollyon wailed. 'The guests are leaving in shoals; you've upset the staff; you've ruined one of the most prestigious conferences we've ever had. *That's* what I appreciate. The cancellations have started coming in already. God alone knows what the long-term consequences will be.'

'We had reason to believe that there might be a professional killer on the premises,' Crozier said. 'A celebrity murder would have been even worse publicity for you.'

'But that's academic, isn't it?' Jollyon, usually the mildest of men, was sufficiently worried to be almost aggressive. 'There was no sign of that *wretched* Veldman woman. I give you fair warning: we shall be laying a formal complaint about this, both to the Tourism Committee and to the Law and Order Committee. We shall consider the possibility of legal action very seriously indeed. I have already been in touch with the owners.'

Crozier abandoned diplomacy. 'You must do as you think fit, Mr Jollyon. Good afternoon.'

He strode out of the office. This débâcle was something else to lay at Bergerac's door. But Crozier was a fair man and, even as the thought came into his head, he realized that Bergerac had acted correctly. With a killer like Veldman on the loose, you couldn't afford to take chances. And the last day of the conference was the last time that Prinknash could be guaranteed to appear in public while he was on Jersey.

The lobby and the Marine Bar were both crowded. People stood and sat in small groups. Most of them looked angry; some of them had already packed their bags. The uniformed inspector who handled public relations for the States Police had been pinned in a corner by five agitated delegates. In front of the reception desk there was a queue of guests waiting restlessly to pay their bills. Jollyon had reason to be angry.

Outside the hotel, the police were in the process of withdrawing. Crozier walked over to his car, brushing aside Claude Yves's attempt to interview him with a brusque 'No comment'. It was mid-afternoon, and he wished it was time to go home. He was having to pay one hell of a price for missing the rest of the conference.

His driver, a saturnine young constable whom Crozier suspected of taking the mickey behind his back, started the engine as soon as he got in the car.

'Just had a message from headquarters, sir. From the top floor. The Superintendent wants to see you.'

It had been a bad afternoon. And it was going to get worse.

Another phone began to ring and Peggy Masters swore at it.

This was exceptional. She was a woman who rarely used what she had been brought up to call 'bad language'. 'Bother!' or 'Oh, blow' sufficed for most situations; 'blast' and 'damn' were reserved for life's crises. This afternoon, however, she muttered the same word as her late husband had used when he hit his thumb with a hammer in the privacy of the garden shed.

At least six phones were ringing; after two or three you

137

lost count. And they had been ringing all afternoon. The entire population of Jersey seemed to be under a compulsion to phone the Bureau. With almost every available man at the Bretagne or the Orchid Factory, she was expected to answer them all. The switchboard in the basement seemed incapable of re-routing the calls.

She lunged at the nearest telephone, which happened to be Bergerac's external line. With all this racket around her, she wasn't sure whether it was ringing or not.

'Bureau des Etrangers,' she snapped. 'What is it?'

'Peggy – it's Susan.'

'Who?' It was difficult to hear anything over the noise of the other phones. She covered her free ear with her hand. 'Can you speak up? . . . Oh, *Susan*. I'm sorry, dear. It's complete chaos here.'

'Any news of Jim?'

'Hasn't he been in touch?' Peggy clicked her tongue against the roof of her mouth. 'That's men all over.'

'He's back, then?'

'Well, I haven't actually seen him. But he flew back from Caen by helicopter. Barry Goddard was going to meet him and take him to the Orchid Factory.'

Susan muttered something under her breath.

'What was that, dear?'

'Nothing.'

Another phone began to ring. Peggy shouted even louder: 'Shall I try to get hold of him? Or can I take a message?'

'No. No message.'

The line went dead.

CHAPTER
15

If you had to do something unpleasant, Crozier believed, it was best to get it over with as soon as possible.

At Rouge Bouillon, he left the Bureau to fend for itself and went straight upstairs. The secretary announced him with a buzz on the intercom and sent him through at once.

The Superintendent was sitting behind the desk; as usual, he seemed completely relaxed to the point of being only half-aware of what was going on around him. The strain was more obvious in Hungerford and Priknash, who were in armchairs round the coffee table. Priknash turned his head sharply as the door opened, and Hungerford jumped to his feet. All of them had been drinking tea from the dainty cups that you only found on the top floor.

Crozier had insisted on Priknash coming directly to headquarters as soon as the Veldman connection emerged. Priknash had agreed only under protest. It was typical of the man that he had refused to be bundled into the waiting police car: he had insisted on driving himself in the Bristol. Hungerford had come too, largely because Crozier had been unable to think of a reason to get rid of him on the spur of the moment.

'I hear you had no luck,' the Superintendent said. His Somerset accent had fooled a lot of people into thinking he thought as slowly and as simply as he spoke. 'Pity. Have a seat.'

'We had to try.' Crozier's voice sounded defensive, even to himself. He sat down on one of the hard chairs, away from the coffee table.

'I won't quarrel with that.' The Superintendent smiled unexpectedly. 'Don't worry, man. You have my full support.'

'Have you heard the news, Barney?' Hungerford interrupted.

'There's been another development, I'm afraid,' the Superintendent said. 'They've found Thornber. With his throat cut.'

'A terrible business,' Prinknash said with a sigh. 'I can't help feeling that in some sense I'm partly responsible.'

'Nonsense, Vernon. These vermin bring it on their own heads.'

The Superintendent raised his eyebrows. 'We've not established that Thornber is guilty of anything, Charlie – except perhaps a little smuggling. Unless you know otherwise?' It was a long speech for him. He allowed a second for the reproof to register and then turned back to Crozier. 'Jim Bergerac's on his way here. Mrs Thornber's collapsed.'

'Two murders,' Hungerford said, 'and an assassin on the loose; *plus* an important visitor who has to behave like he's a prisoner. As you know, Barney, I believe in plain speaking. I think I can speak for the whole of the Committee. It's just not a satisfactory record.'

The intercom buzzed again, just as Crozier was about to say something he would later regret to Hungerford.

'Sergeant Bergerac,' the secretary's disembodied voice said. 'Shall I ask him to wait, sir?'

The Superintendent glanced from Crozier to Hungerford before replying, 'No, send him in.'

When the door opened he made no comment on Bergerac's appearance; the fitness or otherwise of Bureau personnel was Crozier's responsibility, and the Superintendent was a scrupulous man. He pointed to a seat.

Hungerford was not so restrained. 'Been in the wars, Jim?'

Bergerac said nothing.

'Anything new on Thornber?' the Superintendent asked.

'Not really, sir. Lejeune's preliminary examination confirms the probability Thornber was murdered. It was messy but technically efficient. We're working on the assumption that he was lured out of the house, perhaps by a telephone call. So far, no witnesses have come forward.'

'I gather you've been to France today.' The Superintendent's voice was carefully neutral: he must have been aware that Bergerac's visit had been both unofficial and irregular but he would make no reference to that in front of outsiders. 'You'd better fill us in.'

Bergerac hesitated; his eyes slid towards the two visitors by the coffee table.

'Carry on, Sergeant,' the Superintendent said gently.

'The French believe that Thornber was heavily involved in a major smuggling organization. He handled the Normandy-to-Jersey stage of the route. As yet, we've no detailed information about the other stages. His charter business gave him a reasonable cover for going to and fro between here and Carteret. It's likely that he regularly used St Vimy's Bay because of its isolated location, and because Mrs Awtry was so rarely there. His former mistress, a Carteret café-owner, is cooperating with the French police. She claims he was using her. We don't know whether Mrs Thornber was involved or not.'

'Wouldn't surprise me in the least,' Hungerford said. 'I always did think it suspicious, the way she expanded the Orchid Factory so fast. And she often sends stuff to the mainland, and – '

'Thornber's mistress,' Bergerac went on, 'identified a photo of Veldman as a mystery woman who spent several days with Thornber at the café last week. Veldman had scarlet fever. The French and Spanish police have traced her route back to Morocco by the trail of infection she left. This ties up with a rumour current in London, that

Veldman fled to North Africa after her escape from jail. According to the same rumour, she was looking for work.'

Prinknash stirred in his chair. 'Forgive me for seeming naïve, but what sort of work would she have in mind?'

Bergerac glanced grimly at him. 'You know her track record: she specializes mainly in contract kidnapping and murder. The theory is that whoever hired her also arranged, maybe indirectly, for Thornber to bring her to Jersey. You're the only person on the island who is known to have received death threats recently. The threats come from the London underworld, which is also the place where Veldman's contacts are. Thornber caught the scarlet fever and we know that he got hold of two courses of antibiotics. One for him and one for Veldman? We can't prove a thing, but we have to work on the assumption that killing you is her reason for coming here.'

'That seems fair enough.' Prinknash sounded mildly interested but unconcerned; he might have been discussing the price of tomatoes in the market. 'But in that case, how does this man Stroat fit in?'

'It's a fact that he was a professional blackmailer.' Bergerac's voice was weary, and he stumbled once or twice as he spoke. 'Maybe he picked up something at the Orchid Factory – he might have just gathered that some illegal cargo was to be landed at St Vimy's Bay, early on Saturday morning. My guess is that he witnessed Veldman and Thornber arriving – and that they saw him. One or both of them killed him.'

'A bit speculative,' the Superintendent said.

Bergerac shrugged. 'I know, sir. But Sir Vernon's life's at risk. We can't wait for proof.'

'What about the attack on you?'

'Again, I've got no proof, but it must have been Veldman. I'd talked to Thornber that day, and been to see his boat. I was getting too close for comfort. Perhaps the fact I arrested her last time had something to do with it, as well:

she has no reason to like me. And there's one little bit of evidence: whoever attacked me was wearing something long and dark; and Thornber hired a nun's habit for a month from a theatrical costumier in Caen. We haven't found the habit, so we're assuming that he got it for Veldman.'

'You think she killed Thornber?' Crozier asked. 'Why?'

'To shut his mouth? He wasn't in her league. My guess is that the murder of Stroat really shook him up. Suddenly he was an accessory to something he couldn't handle. He was the one person who could betray her.'

'Where's she been hiding?' Prinknash asked. 'At the Orchid Factory? She must be somewhere.'

'I agree it's the obvious place, but we've found no sign of her yet. We'll keep looking. Personally, I don't think Thornber would have risked having her there. His wife's no fool. Most days there's a cleaning woman at the house, and anyway he was so ill he couldn't have done much to look after her. And the staff at the Factory noticed nothing there or in the grounds.'

'So maybe he found her somewhere else,' Crozier suggested. 'He could have set it up before he brought her here.'

Bergerac nodded. 'It's worth following up. Unless she breaks cover and tries to leave or kill Sir Vernon, it's our best bet. I don't see how else we can trace her.'

'Estate agents,' Crozier said, 'small hotels, bed-and-breakfasts, camp-sites and private lets. It'll take a lot of manpower.'

'Maybe we should talk to Mrs Thornber again,' Bergerac said. 'Even if she isn't involved, she might remember something her husband did or said that could give us a handle on where Veldman's staying.'

'OK – give it a try.' The Superintendent turned back to Crozier. 'Of course we'll need the island-wide search as well. You can draft in men from other departments.'

Hungerford cleared his throat. 'I suppose you'll be

leaving Jersey now,' he said to Prinknash. 'No reason to stay, really, now the conference is over. You've . . . er, you've made your point, you know. Refused to be intimidated and so forth.'

Prinknash grinned. 'Not throwing me out, are you, Charlie?'

'Of course not, Vernon. You can stay as long as you like.' Hungerford hesitated before adding, rather gloomily, 'Naturally, it's a pleasure to have you.'

'The thing is, I originally planned to stay until Saturday – until Miss Veldman's – ah – self-imposed deadline expires.' He waved a long, graceful hand. 'I apologize for the pun, gentlemen.'

'You'd be safer in London,' the Superintendent said. 'Scotland Yard have better facilities to handle this sort of thing. And, of course, a lot more experience with it than we have.'

'Frankly, I'm not sure that I would be safer.' Prinknash smiled at the Superintendent. 'I've been very impressed by what I've seen of the States Police. But that's not the point. I was hoping to do a bit more fishing. I don't see why I should change my plans just because some psychopathic hoodlum is making wild threats. It goes against the grain.'

'I can't force you to leave, sir. But I'd feel much happier if you did.'

'I shall, Superintendent. But in my own good time.'

'Then I must insist that wherever you go on this island, you go in convoy with a police escort. I'm going to double the previous level of protection. You'll trip over a policeman every time you go to the loo.'

Their eyes met. For a moment Crozier thought that Prinknash was going to argue. Then the two men smiled at one another, as though each had recognized the other as a worthy adversary. The tension dissolved. It occurred to Crozier that, beneath the surface differences of background and appearance, Prinknash and the Superintendent had a lot of similarities: both men masked their power with courtesy; both had been decorated for bravery; and both were as difficult to deflect as a guided missile.

Prinknash switched the charm to his unwilling host. 'Charlie, I'm sorry. I'm putting you in an intolerable position. I'll move into the Bretagne or somewhere for the last two nights.'

'Not at all,' Hungerford said awkwardly. 'I wouldn't hear of it. You're staying with me.'

'I'd prefer it if you did stay with Mr Hungerford, sir,' Crozier said. 'It'll mean fewer security headaches for us.'

'All those policemen must be costing Charlie a fortune in teabags and biscuits,' Prinknash said with a chuckle. 'But if he can put up with me, I'd like to stay.'

The Superintendent looked at his watch. 'Is that everything?'

Bergerac leant forward. 'There's one other thing, sir.'

The Superintendent pushed back his chair. 'Is it important, Jim?'

'I don't know. It might be. A retired clergyman went missing a couple of days ago, over in Gorey. A Mr Wetherby.'

'Well, what's the connection?'

The others were on their feet. Crozier was already standing by the door, impatient to get things moving.

'Isn't Wetherby a friend of yours?' he said.

Bergerac nodded. 'But that's got nothing to do with it. The point is, another retired priest thought that Wetherby walked off with a nun. Admittedly he's not a reliable witness.'

'Coincidence,' Crozier said shortly. 'You've got nuns on the brain.'

'There's no link between Veldman and Wetherby?' the Superintendent asked.

'None that we've found.'

'Then it looks like Barney's right. A coincidence.'

*

145

By four o'clock, Susan had had enough.

The third phone call from Mrs Elsted left her drained of energy but full of rage. She knew very well that she was using Mrs Elsted as a substitute for Jim. She decided to cut her losses and go home.

First, however, she was going to call at the bungalow. Apley and Tuke still hadn't been in touch. She wasn't even sure that their representative was at the bungalow. He certainly wasn't answering the phone or replying to the notes she had pushed into the letter-box. Apart from the car parked outside the bungalow on Saturday afternoon, she had seen no sign of occupation.

The situation was impossible; and it was wasting far too much of her precious time. Hobson and Young made it a matter of policy to respect the privacy of their tenants, but the time had come to be pragmatic. The agency carried spare sets of keys for all the properties they managed. She grabbed the keys for the bungalow and left the office. She was aware that Tim Hobson watched her departure with interest.

Her route to Maufant took her through Rouge Bouillon. To her irritation, there was a hold-up near police head-quarters. Uniformed policemen halted the traffic in both directions. Other officers patrolled the pavements, glancing inside the waiting vehicles.

Susan rolled down her window. 'What's going on?'

A young constable came over to her; he had a freckled face and looked about fifteen.

'Routine security exercise, madam,' he said with the self-importance of the very young. 'Won't keep you long.'

A large motorcade swept out of the entrance and turned north. All the pomp and circumstance suggested that the cause was visiting royalty at the very least. There were five cars and a swarm of motor-cyclists. One of the cars was familiar. Susan frowned in the effort to remember where she had seen it.

The traffic began to move again. The driver behind her honked his horn. The memory slid suddenly into place in Susan's mind: it was the same large, grey car that she had seen outside the bungalow in Maufant on Saturday afternoon. She glanced across the road. Bergerac and Wilson were coming down the steps from one entrance.

On impulse she pulled over to the kerb and parked on a yellow line. The driver behind missed her rear bumper by inches. She jumped out of the jeep and ran across the road.

'Jim!'

A few yards away, the freckled constable tensed. Maybe he thought she was a potential terrorist.

Bergerac looked up, waved and walked on.

At the last moment, even anger failed her. Susan dashed after him into the police car park, and caught his arm. He looked like one of the walking wounded in a bad war movie.

'Are you all right?' she heard herself saying.

'Sue – I'm sorry. But I have to go.'

'Jim, we're short of vehicles,' Wilson interrupted. 'Where's your car?'

'It's at Susan's,' Bergerac said. 'Get a lift from Pettit. We'll pick it up as we go.'

Susan took a deep breath. 'Why the hell aren't you – '

'There's no time for this.' Bergerac took her arm. 'You said you'd seen Wetherby at a solicitor's, the other day. Where?'

'It was Roger Rimmer,' she said automatically. 'But – '

'I'll see you later.' He was already climbing into the waiting police car. 'Take care.'

The car pulled away from her. She was standing outside police headquarters with the tears spilling out of her eyes. She had even forgotten to ask him about the grey car – not that he would have had time to answer. The bungalow keys slipped from her hand. She bent down to pick them up.

For the first time she noticed the label attached to the ring. The keys belonged to another property they handled in Maufant. In her hurry to leave, she must have picked up the wrong set.

This was definitely not her day. She had the wrong keys and the wrong man. She asked the wrong questions and got the wrong answers.

She looked down at the keys. There was something she could get right. Even if it killed her.

CHAPTER
16

Pettit double-parked beside the Triumph Roadster. He braked so suddenly that Bergerac and Wilson were jerked forward.

'Here we are, Sarge,' he said. 'Fastest taxi in town.'

He pulled away with a screech of rubber as soon as his passengers were out of the back of the car.

Wilson stared after him. 'Who does he think he is?' he said sourly. 'Jersey's answer to – '

'Drop it, Terry,' Bergerac said, fumbling in his pocket for the car keys. 'He's seen them drive like that on TV.' He unlocked the driver's door.

Wilson frowned. 'You shouldn't be driving. Let me do it.'

Bergerac climbed carefully into the car. At present, all his movements were careful: he couldn't be entirely sure that his muscles would do what he required of them.

He had taken another dose of painkillers at the Bureau, along with several glasses of water to ease the sore throat. His head was muzzy and Wilson's voice sounded slightly distorted, as though he was speaking with his mouth full. But nothing was actually hurting very much. That was progress.

He looked up at Wilson. 'I've got another job for you.'

'I thought we were going to the Orchid Factory.'

'I am. But you're staying in St Helier. I want you to go to Don Road and try and get someone to talk to you.'

'Is it to do with Thornber?'

'Maybe. In a way.'

'Then why wait till now to tell me?'

Bergerac shrugged and put the key in the ignition.

'I get it.' Wilson's mouth set in a hard line. He bent down so that his face was level with Bergerac's. 'Because you didn't want anyone else to know. Because someone's put this off-limits. And it's a pound to a penny that the someone just happens to be Barney Crozier.'

'You're letting your imagination run away with you,' Bergerac said coldly. 'I don't want any argument Terry, OK? I'm not in the mood.'

'You're not even on duty – '

'Don't be so bloody silly. You saw what's happening at the Bureau: we're in the middle of an all-island alert, and Crozier needs everyone he can get. So my sick leave is temporarily cancelled. I'm back on the strength. You're going to argue the toss with him?'

Wilson scowled. 'The point is – '

'The point is, I'm a DS and you're just a DC. Right now that means if I want you to do something, you damn well do it.' Bergerac jerked his head away so Wilson could not see the agony on his face. The pain was searing but mercifully brief. 'Sorry,' he said, looking up again. 'I didn't mean to take it out on you.'

'That's OK,' Wilson said grudgingly.

'Just do what I say, all right? This could be important.' Bergerac hesitated, hoping that he was right to trust Wilson; if he was wrong, he would just be providing Crozier with more ammunition against him. But it was too late to weigh the odds. 'Terry, you're going to have to be diplomatic because we haven't much leverage here. It's a long shot and it's not going to be easy, but this is what I want you to do.'

'Back again?' Tim Hobson said. 'I thought we'd seen the last of you for this afternoon.'

'So did I.' Susan strode to the rear of the office. 'I took the wrong set of keys.'

'They wouldn't be for the bungalow, by any chance? In Maufant?'

'Yes. Why?'

Susan picked up the correct keys and double-checked the label.

'Because Mrs Elsted phoned just after you left.' Hobson straightened a set of house details on one of the display racks and stood back to admire his handiwork. 'I flatter myself I handled her rather well.'

'Did she actually have anything to say?'

'She had this brilliant idea: why don't we ask the police to help us with the bungalow. Apart from that, she brought me up to date about her niece, and gave me a consumer guide to the shopping facilities in Worthing. Oh, and she made some rather cutting comments about Apley and Tuke.'

'I tried the police,' Susan said grimly, 'in a manner of speaking. About ten minutes ago.'

'But surely – oh, you mean you asked Jim?' Hobson's face brightened with interest; he knew that Bergerac had made an illicit departure from his sickbed. 'So he's back now, is he?'

'Not as far as I'm concerned.' Susan's voice was bitter. 'The Bureau's in the middle of some sort of panic. I saw him outside police headquarters, but the last thing he had time for was talking to me. I wasn't even able to ask him about the grey car.'

'What grey car? And how could Jim help?'

Suddenly Hobson's curiosity seemed almost prurient; he was too fond of acting the Agony Aunt. What he really wanted to find out was what had happened in the latest instalment of the Susan-and-Jim saga.

Susan shrugged and said, 'What does it matter? It might have been the same car I saw outside the bungalow.'

'But I'm interested, Susan.' His voice was almost a wail. 'It's only natural that – ' His phone cut him off in mid sentence. He snatched it up. 'Hobson and Young. Can I help you?'

Susan made good her escape. As she left the office, she glanced back. Hobson was handling an enquiry with his usual charm and efficiency. He was also staring at her, and his eyes were reproachful.

'Go easy on her, Jim,' Dr Fender said. 'And go easy on yourself, too. You look terrible.'

'But it's OK to see her?'

Fender shrugged. 'As her GP, I'd prefer you didn't. But I suppose in the circumstances you have to. No more than ten minutes, mind. Make it five if you can.'

He climbed into his Volkswagen. The car sank beneath his weight. The engine started with the sort of full-throated roar that suggests that the silencer is about to drop off. He drove jerkily down the drive like an automated kangaroo.

Bergerac and Goddard climbed the steps to the front door. By now, Thornber's body had been removed to the mortuary, but there was still a good deal of police activity in the grounds. The scene-of-the-crime team was picking its way, inch by inch, through the belt of firs. Other men were combing the gardens. The house and the Orchid Factory had already been searched. So far they had found no sign of Norma Jean Veldman. Bergerac would be surprised if they did. Veldman wasn't stupid.

Inside, the house seemed precisely as it had been when Bergerac was last here. Death had left no obvious blemish on it. In the hall there were fresh flowers whose scent mingled with polish. A uniformed constable, who had been sprawling in one of the chairs by the fireplace, hastily stood up as they came in.

Goddard gestured to the stairs. 'She's in her bedroom with a WPC. Fender gave her a sedative.'

Mrs Thornber's room was smaller than her husband's. It was sparsely furnished in comparison with the muted luxury of the reception rooms downstairs. The window faced north, and the impression of gloom was increased by the heavy, dark-stained wardrobe and the matching chest-of-drawers. The only sign of personal indulgence was a row of tinted eighteenth-century prints on one wall; they were a set of six, depicting different kinds of orchids.

The WPC was sitting bolt upright on a hard chair beside the single bed. The inevitable tea tray stood on a small table. Mary Thornber lay propped up against the pillows, fully dressed except for her shoes. Her hands were locked together: she was playing with her wedding ring.

Bergerac and Goddard hovered in the doorway. The woman on the bed stared at them with dull, incurious eyes. At a nod from Bergerac, the WPC stood up and backed away from her chair.

'We'd like to ask you a few questions, Mrs Thornber,' Bergerac said. 'Is that OK?'

The eyes wandered to the window. 'Ask anything you want,' she said harshly. 'I haven't any answers.'

Bergerac lacked the time and energy that a subtle and tactful approach required. He blundered straight in: 'We're trying to trace your husband's killer. We suspect that a woman is involved, and that he may have arranged a hiding-place for her sometime last week.'

'Of course there's a woman involved.' Her head moved restlessly on the pillow. 'Jack thought I didn't know. It's been going on for months. Perfume on his shirts. That smug look on his face when he got back from overnight trips. I know the signs. I should do by this time.'

'This is a different woman. She – '

Mrs Thornber continued, in the same low monotonous voice, as though he hadn't spoken. 'He was a bad lot, Sergeant. That's the long and the short of it. Lazy, too. But I was used to him, you see. And sometimes . . . sometimes it was handy to have a man about the house. It's strange how . . .'

As she hesitated, searching for words, Bergerac seized the chance to interrupt. 'Were there any unusual phone calls for your husband last week? Any letters?'

Mrs Thornber frowned, as if resenting the intrusion on her train of thought. Deliberately she turned away and addressed the WPC. 'But now I wonder if I drove him to it. At the beginning, when I started the business, there was so little time. I used to work eighteen-hour days. And he must have been very vulnerable then, just after his firm had failed. I can see that now. He had needs, and I couldn't fulfil them. Couldn't? Wouldn't? What do you think? I don't know.'

Her tone, if not her words, had a dreadful familiarity to all her listeners. This was one of the common consequences of sudden death: the survivors were condemned to a bitter process of self-examination – bitter because it was too late to profit by the results, and because the guilt it engendered could never be expiated.

There was a chair by the door. Bergerac sat down suddenly.

'Had he got a friend with an empty house?' he said wearily. 'An empty boat, even?'

'Friend?' Mrs Thornber gazed vacantly at him, turning the word over in her mind. 'Jack doesn't – didn't – have friends. Just drinking partners and business associates. When we met, that was something I liked about him. He seemed self-sufficient, like me. Or rather, like I thought I was. I thought that marriage would be him and me against the world. An alliance of equals.' She bit her lip. 'Do you think he loved me?'

This question had to be answered. Bergerac mumbled, 'I'm sure he did.'

'He might have done.' Mrs Thornber nodded, conceding that it was possible, if unlikely. 'But I doubt it. I think he wanted my money to prop up his business. He didn't get it, of course. I'm not a fool. No point in throwing away good money after bad.'

'Mrs Thornber, I want you to answer this question: where do you think your husband might have hidden this woman?'

The sudden harshness of Bergerac's voice had two effects: the WPC stirred and took a step towards her charge; and Mrs Thornber tugged the wedding ring from her finger and threw it on the floor. The ring rolled in an arc and came to rest against Bergerac's foot. Goddard stooped, picked it up and put it on the chest.

'If I had done that years ago,' she went on, 'maybe he would still be alive. He would have married someone else and none of this need have happened. I killed him.'

The WPC shot an angry glance at Bergerac and sat down on the edge of the bed. She took Mrs Thornber's hand.

'Now that's being silly, dear,' she said brightly. 'It's like wishing you hadn't been born so you wouldn't have to die.' She hesitated, as if aware that there might be something wrong with the analogy. 'Now, why don't you have a nice cup of tea?'

Bergerac stood up. He and Goddard slipped out of the room without saying goodbye. On their way downstairs they heard the sound of breaking china.

'Mr Rimmer doesn't see *anyone* without an appointment,' the secretary said firmly.

Wilson produced his warrant card. 'Come on, love,' he said. 'I'm in a bit of a hurry, and this is important.'

'But someone's with him. I can't disturb him. He hates that.'

'He won't mind, I promise.' Wilson smiled at the girl, which was easy to do; Rimmer had good taste in secretaries. 'He's a solicitor, isn't he?'

'Of course he is.' She glanced up at him. She wasn't

thawing, but she was puzzled. 'But what's that got to do with it?'

'Solicitors generally like to get on with the police,' he said gently. 'It's what you might call a fact of professional life.'

For an instant he thought he had pitched it a bit strong. Then her puzzled expression gave way to a look of doubt. She had a new question to answer: which would make Rimmer angrier – being disturbed in the middle of a meeting or offending a copper unnecessarily?

Wilson glanced at the nameplate beside her typewriter. He lowered his voice. 'I shouldn't be telling you this, Elaine,' he said conspiratorially. 'But I'm on a murder enquiry.'

Her eyes widened. 'Who's been killed? It's not about that man Stroat, is it? The one that's been in the papers?'

Wilson winked. 'Let's say there may be a connection.'

Her hand hesitated over the phone. 'He won't like this, you know.'

'He'll like it even less if I don't see him.'

She picked up the phone and buzzed Rimmer. Wilson tried and failed to hear what was said at the other end. He noticed there was an intercom on her desk; presumably she thought the phone would be more discreet.

Elaine covered the mouthpiece. 'He can see you in five to ten minutes. Can you wait?' Her eyes travelled over him with interest. 'I could make you some tea, if you want.'

Wilson grinned at her. 'I'll wait. It'll be a pleasure.'

'Nothing, Barney. A total waste of time. They've drawn a blank everywhere.'

'What about the widow?' Crozier said.

Bergerac lowered his voice, though he knew that only Goddard could hear him. He was phoning in a small room that was furnished as a study. 'It was pointless even trying.

Doctor Fender had pumped something into her, and in any case she was off her head with grief.'

Crozier grunted. Mrs Thornber's grief didn't concern him; the absence of hard information did. 'We've not got any further this end,' he said. 'We've checked all the hotels in the first register, and most of the ones in the second. I've even tried the convents, just in case. But the guest-houses are the real nightmare. There's something like 250 of them.'

'What do you want us to do?' Bergerac asked. 'Cover the guest-houses at the St Brelade end?'

'No – you'd better make a start on the estate agents. Only about fifty of those.'

'Barney – do you think I could recruit some outside help on this? Get some expert advice?'

'You mean Susan?' Crozier said suspiciously.

'Well, why not? You know what estate agents are – one of these professional mafias. Maybe she and Tim Hobson could help short-circuit the checks. For a start, they'd know the main agencies that handle holiday lets.'

'All right. Just advice, though. No cowboy stuff, OK? We're not going to swear them in as Special Constables and issue them with handcuffs.'

'Scout's honour,' Bergerac said. These painkillers did something to his sense of humour: sometimes he had an almost irresistible urge to giggle. The thought of Susan as a Special Constable was too much for him to cope with in his present state.

'One more thing, Jim. I've not forgotten about this morning. Don't think you won't have to answer for that when all this is over.'

Crozier put down the phone. Bergerac no longer had any desire to laugh. Sometimes these painkillers made him feel that he would never be able to laugh again.

*

'Detective Constable Wilson?' Rimmer held out his hand; he liked to start on a cordial footing with policemen. 'I don't think we've met, have we?'

'No, sir.'

The outer door of the office closed behind a formidable African woman who was determined to buy her way into a Jersey consortium. The lady's determination suggested that it could be a profitable relationship, and Rimmer was sorry to see her go.

He ushered Wilson into his private office and closed the door. 'The Bureau des Etrangers? I know Chief Inspector Crozier quite well.'

He glanced at his visitor, hoping that the policeman was not too dim to take such an obvious hint: *If you're wasting my time, your boss is going to hear about it.*

'We share a hobby, actually,' he went on. 'Flying model aircraft. Do sit down. Now, what can I do for you?'

Even seated, Wilson's bulk dominated the little room. 'Well, sir. It's about one of your clients.'

Rimmer held up his hand. 'Before you go on, I should make it clear that I may not be able to answer your questions if they relate to a particular client. Professional ethics, you know.'

'Yes, sir,' said Wilson woodenly. 'Your ethics cover murder enquiries, do they?'

'Naturally that depends on circumstances.'

Rimmer spent two minutes explaining precisely why. The mention of murder had been a shock – he preferred not to deal with criminal cases at all, if he could help it; but on the other hand, he had no intention of being bullied by a lumpish constable. The sound of his own voice, fluently describing the solicitor's code of conduct in terms that even this layman could be expected to understand, gradually had a soothing effect on him.

'The client in question,' Wilson interrupted as Rimmer

paused before his peroration, 'is the Reverend Robert Wetherby. I take it he is one of your clients, sir?'

Rimmer blinked, temporarily thrown off balance by the direct question. 'Yes he is, as a matter of fact. Why?'

'He's not been seen since Tuesday afternoon.'

'How odd. I wonder ... I was on the verge of ringing him, in fact. I've been rather surprised that he hasn't been in touch.'

'What was he seeing you about?'

Rimmer smiled, and said with a carefully-judged touch of condescension: 'I'm not convinced that is any of your business, constable.'

'It's the possible link with a murder investigation that – '

'But what murder? And what's the link?' Rimmer was gathering momentum again. He was a small man and large men often made him irritable. 'Frankly, it seems rather unlikely that Wetherby could be mixed up with ... something like that. You're not suggesting that *he's* been killed, I take it?'

'No, sir, not as far as we know. But his disappearance has been officially reported to us – '

'To the Bureau? How strange. I understood that Mr Wetherby is a resident.'

'To the police.' Wilson, his enormous hands planted on his equally enormous knees, refused to be harried. 'But there may be a connection with a murder case. I'm not at liberty to tell you the nature of that connection.'

'The tourist?' Rimmer said quickly. 'Stroat? That's the only recent murder of a visitor that I can recall.'

Wilson nodded.

'This mysterious connection,' Rimmer went on. 'Are you saying that the dead man knew Mr Wetherby?'

Wilson coughed politely. 'I'm not saying anything at all about it, sir. What I'd like to know is the nature of the business you're handling for Mr Wetherby. Would it be his will, perhaps?'

Rimmer looked consideringly across his desk. If the police really wanted to know, they would get it out of him sooner or later. Wetherby could scarcely object to the breach of confidence, not in these circumstances. No doubt the police would be discreet. But it went against Rimmer's grain to be too helpful too soon.

'No – he made a will some time ago, I believe. Before he came to me. It was a business matter. The disposal of a capital sum.'

Wilson frowned. 'I understood that Mr Wetherby isn't a rich man. In fact he's more or less living on charity, isn't he?'

'Oh no, constable.' Rimmer sat back, enjoying his moment of triumph. 'At a rough guess – very rough, of course – I would say that Mr Wetherby is one of the ten most wealthy men on Jersey.'

CHAPTER
17

Tim Hobson's eyes gleamed. 'Good lord,' he said. 'You look as if a puff of wind would blow you away.'

Bergerac looked round the estate agency. 'Where's Susan? Is she here?'

'She's gone out, I'm afraid. Just a small job – she said she'd be going straight home afterwards. Anything I can do?'

'Yes. Can we talk in private?'

Hobson led him into the small office at the back. Bergerac leant against the desk because his legs were trembling. The absence of Susan was an unexpectedly bitter disappointment. He had hoped that asking for her assistance might help to bridge the gap between them. But that was a purely personal side-issue. Hobson would do just as well as far as the main purpose of his visit was concerned.

'We're trying to trace a woman who's hiding out on the island. She's an escaped convict, and she's a killer. Her name's Norma Jean Veldman.'

'I know,' Hobson said, his face alight with interest. 'The one who escaped by helicopter.'

'That's her. She's been on Jersey for the best part of a week. She must have a base somewhere. We don't think she's staying with friends. So we're checking hotels and so on. But there's another possibility: she may have found herself some sort of self-catering holiday let. Even leased a house, for all we know. And that's where you come in. I don't just mean your own leases – I've got to check every estate agent on the island, plus every private person who handles their own property.'

'Well, I can let you have a list of the main firms, and the people there who deal with short-term lets: that's no problem. And we can easily check our own files, here and now.'

'We're short of time and we're short of men,' Bergerac said. 'Could you do some of the phoning for me?'

Hobson nodded happily. 'It'd be a pleasure, Jim.' He opened a filing cabinet and began to flick through the contents.

'Veldman may be disguised as a nun,' Bergerac went on. 'There's another point: she might have arranged the let through a third party.'

'There's a flat in Gorey.' Hobson pulled out a folder and tossed it on the desk. 'A retired couple took it at the end of April. We've got two old ladies in a place in Marett Road.' A second folder joined the first. 'Oh, and there's the bungalow in Maufant. In fact Susan's . . .'

The excitement drained away from Hobson's face. It took Bergerac a second to identify the emotions that replaced it.

Surprise, and then – ?

Hobson's plump, good-natured features were ill-adapted for showing anxiety. He licked his lips.

'Jim, there's something odd about that lease. It's a three-month let to a London firm, Apley and Tuke. The owner's leaning on us to change the terms of the lease but we haven't been able to get through to them at all.'

'What's the address?' Bergerac snapped.

Hobson scribbled it on a piece of paper, continuing to speak as he wrote: 'No one's available at their London office. Susan's phoned the bungalow, she's left messages there, but we haven't had an answer and so she took the duplicate keys and – '

'She's there now?' Bergerac snatched the sheet of paper.

'Get on to Crozier at the Bureau. Tell him what you've told me.'

He ran through the outer office, pushing his way through a knot of browsers. Hobson plunged after him. Just before the door, Bergerac stumbled and collided with one of the stands. He recovered his balance but the stand toppled sideways, blocking Hobson's path and sending a shower of property details on to the carpet.

Hobson picked himself up. 'Jim, there was something else – '

The door swung shut with a hiss of compressed air. Bergerac scrambled into the Triumph without bothering to open the car's door. The engine fired. Hobson charged on to the pavement.

'Jim,' he gasped, 'Susan was going to ask you about a grey car she'd seen leaving the Bureau. It was at the bungalow . . .'

The Triumph roared forward, drowning the rest of Hobson's words. He wondered if anything he had said had got through to Bergerac. The little car pushed into the stream of traffic and rapidly accelerated. Horns blared, adding to the din.

'Jim! Wait a moment!'

Hobson's voice began as a shout but ended as a whisper. Even as he spoke, he knew it was too late.

The Triumph shot through a red light, turned right with a squeal of brakes and disappeared.

'It's an extraordinary will.' Rimmer's professional distaste was obvious from his face. 'But it's perfectly valid. Watertight, too. Mr Wetherby is the sole heir.'

Wilson looked up from his notebook. 'Who was this man Scowles? I've never heard of him.'

'Not many people have. I believe he started out as a cockney barrow-boy. But he had an interest in radio. This was just after the First World War. Radio was the new technology of the 1920s. Scowles started out in a back room in Hoxton. He was young enough to understand the product and he was good at selling it. He also spotted the military potential early on. Got a few War Office contracts in the 1930s. Then the thing really snowballed in the last war: he ended up a millionaire. That was when a million pounds really meant something. He sold up to a multi-national in the early fifties and just sat back and watched his money grow.'

'So why wasn't he better known?'

Rimmer shrugged. 'He never liked publicity. He hid himself behind the usual corporate fronts. Wetherby told me that Scowles was shy. Judging by the terms of the will, I'd call him cynical and misanthropic to the point of paranoia.'

Wilson turned over the page. 'What was the connection between him and Wetherby?'

'Eh?' Rimmer steepled his fingers. 'Don't you think it might be fair to tell me something first? A *quid pro quo*, as we lawyers say. For example, what's the link between Stroat and Mr Wetherby?'

'We're in the early stages of the investigation, sir,' Wilson said awkwardly. 'It's difficult to be precise.'

'I'm sure you have an idea.'

Wilson hesitated, weighing the necessity for discretion against the need to keep Rimmer talking. 'We believe Mr Wetherby was last seen in the company of a certain person,' he said carefully. 'It's possible that the same person was responsible for killing Stroat.'

'I hope he's all right,' Rimmer said suddenly. 'Wetherby, I mean.' His cheeks were pink. 'I . . . I rather like him, you know.'

'Yes, sir. Scowles and Wetherby?'

'Mr Wetherby spent most of his working life in parishes in the East End. I understand that, before the war, he helped Scowles' mother in some way. There's something

164

else in the will.' Rimmer opened the folder that lay before him on the desk. 'Here we are: "I have chosen Robert Wetherby because he is the only good man I have ever met. Another point in his favour is that he will not want the money. It will be a burden to him, and for that reason he is unlikely to do much harm with it. Frankly, I do not care in the slightest how he uses it."' Rimmer sighed. 'As I said, an extraordinary document. Scowles used one of these will-forms you buy from stationers. But it's clear and incontest-able, and there are no relatives to fight it. He deposited the will, in a sealed envelope, with his solicitors. They con-tacted Mr Wetherby after Scowles died. And he came to me.'

'What does Mr Wetherby want to do with the money?'

Rimmer sighed. 'He wants to give it away. Every last penny. I've tried to reason with him, believe me. I'm in the middle of drawing up the papers. It's an immensely com-plicated job.'

'I suppose he can do what he likes. After all, it's his.'

'Yes, but – I don't know, generosity on that scale is so *unsettling* for the rest of us,' Rimmer said in a burst of candour that surprised himself as much as his visitor. 'I mean, one's just not used to that sort of thing.'

'Especially not on Jersey,' Wilson said dryly. He won-dered how big a bill Wetherby would have to pay for Rimmer's professional services. 'Where's the money going to?'

Rimmer leafed through the file and pulled out another sheet of paper. 'The General Hospital will get a very substantial donation. One or two local charities, including the Halton Home, are getting a few thousand apiece. And the residue will be divided between Help the Aged, Save the Children and Oxfam. It will all take time, of course. The executor is in the process of realizing Scowles' assets. He was Scowles' solicitor. As a matter of fact – '

'I have to ask if anyone would stand to benefit if Mr

Wetherby died before he'd got rid of the money. And could anyone prevent him from giving it away?'

A guarded expression crossed Rimmer's face. 'I must stress how confidential this is. Mr Wetherby was most insistent about that, right from the start. He doesn't want anyone to know that he's got the money. And a condition of all the donations is that the donor is to remain anonymous.'

'I understand that, sir. We're used to keeping our mouths shut.' Wilson looked surreptitiously at his watch. 'But can you answer my questions?'

Rimmer ran his fingers through his hair. 'Look, I don't know for certain, but I think that Mr Wetherby has a reason for wanting to be anonymous. Don't quote me, it's just a hunch.' Rimmer stared unhappily at Wilson. 'It's just that once or twice I've tried to find out if Wetherby had any close relations who might have some sort of moral claim on him. Even a legal one. And each time I tried, he froze up on me. The defences went up. I know it doesn't sound very much, but it means a hell of a lot to anyone who knows Wetherby. The whole question of family is something he's scared of.'

'Who are you?' Susan said.

The nun smiled. 'I think I might ask you the same question.'

'I'm from Hobson and Young, the owner's agents.' Susan saw her letters on the hall table; they had been opened. 'I've been trying to get in touch with Apley and Tuke or their representative on the island. But what are you doing here?'

The nun was a big woman and she dominated the little hall. Her arms were folded across her chest. Behind her, one of the bedroom doors was slightly ajar. The bungalow smelled stuffy as if no one had opened the windows for a while. Someone had been smoking. Surely nuns weren't allowed cigarettes?

'My brother works for Apley and Tuke,' the nun said. 'I'm just visiting.'

'Is he here?'

'No, I'm afraid not. Do you want to leave a message?'

Something stirred in the bedroom. The wind? *But the windows are closed.*

Susan said, 'He's obviously had my letters . . .'

'I know he's been very busy,' the nun said soothingly. 'I'm sure he'll be in touch. I'll tell him you called.'

Someone groaned.

Their eyes met. The nun's, Susan noticed, were small but very blue. Susan had a sour taste in her mouth. She took an involuntary step forward. There was another groan.

'What was that?'

The nun said nothing. With a sudden movement she unfolded her arms. The full sleeves of her habit swung back. Metal gleamed in her right hand.

Susan thought: *But this can't be happening.*

She backed away automatically. When her back reached the wall, there was nowhere left to go.

The knife lunged forward until the tip touched Susan's throat.

Time had suddenly run out.

As he drove the radio crackled. Wilson was talking. Bergerac couldn't concentrate. Words filtered through – fragments of sentences that, put together, made a mosaic of sense. But a substantial part of the picture was still missing. He knew that the case was incomplete, but for once it didn't matter; he hadn't time to think like a policeman. Only Susan mattered. He hoped to God he was overreacting.

A grey car? Had Hobson really said that, or was he imagining it?

Driving was hard enough. The car was acting strangely: it swayed from side to side. He clipped a parked lorry on the outskirts of St Helier, scraping the Triumph's wing along its bumper. *Concentrate on driving.* He should be making plans. But there wasn't time for that, either.

'The executor's another connection,' Wilson was saying. 'It's got to mean something . . .'

Of course it means something. It means a new dimension to the case. It means that Robert Wetherby is in danger, if he isn't dead already. But the point is that Susan –

Bergerac changed down to overtake a van. A Ford Fiesta was coming in the opposite direction. He ignored it. Both the van and the oncoming car had to brake sharply to avoid collision. But the Triumph was through, and the road ahead was clear.

'. . . And there's something strange about his family,' Wilson said. 'Jim? Are you there?'

Good question, Terry. Here and there and all stations between . . .

'Jim? Do you read me?'

Bergerac reached across and switched off the radio. It wasn't a conscious decision. Wilson's voice was a distraction he couldn't afford.

Something was wrong with him. His body encased him like an ill-fitting suit of armour, and each muscle had its individual ache. Everything – from the familiar road to the dashboard in front of him – had an alien quality, as though he had stumbled by accident into another Jersey on another planet. He was going mad. Maybe he had swallowed too many painkillers. Had Dr Lejeune said anything about side-effects? Bergerac couldn't remember.

In Maufant he turned left. He saw the bungalow almost immediately. Susan's jeep was parked in the little drive. The relief was so great that tears pricked against his eyelids. *She's here. I've found her.*

He roared in second gear up the narrow access road. The

rev-counter's needle flickered into the red. He braked just in time to avoid ramming the jeep. The engine stalled.

Then he was running up the path to the bungalow. The front door was locked. Its top panel was filled with a pane of frosted glass that had an endlessly repeated pattern of tiny sailing boats.

A black figure moved on the other side of the glass.

The nun?

Bergerac backed away from the door. On the left of the drive was a small rockery. He pulled out a fist-sized chunk of granite and lobbed it through the nearest window.

It was a sash window, the two halves held in place by the usual snib. He thrust his hand through the hole and unlatched it. His wrist was painful. He withdrew the hand and lifted the lower half of the window. Blood ran down his jacket and splashed on to the sill. He scrambled headfirst through the gap and rolled into the room. The impact penetrated the protective shield of the drugs, and he shouted with pain.

He scrambled to his feet, steadying himself against the back of a sofa. The door was closed. The piece of granite lay in the middle of the carpet. Bergerac picked it up.

Apart from the rasp of his breathing, the bungalow was silent. Veldman must have heard the sound of breaking glass. So where was she? He opened the door as quietly as he could. The hall was empty. A wall-clock ticked above the table. All but one of the other doors were closed.

Perhaps he had imagined the black figure. He could be hallucinating. Anything was possible. *Those damned pain-killers.* Blood dripped on to the parquet floor. That was real.

He tiptoed across the hall and pushed open the door that was ajar. Immediately opposite him was a cupboard. The first thing he saw was Robert Wetherby: there was blood on his face, and he was slumped on the floor of the cupboard.

Alive or dead?

Bergerac's eyes travelled round the room. Susan was sitting bolt-upright on a hard chair at the end of the bed. Her arms and legs were lashed to the chair with wire. She was gagged. Her face was so pale that the freckles almost glowed with colour.

'Sue – '

The granite fell from his hand and thudded on the carpet. The need to help her overrode every other consideration; it was not a conscious decision on his part. He ran forward and knelt beside the chair. His fingers tugged impotently at the wire. She strained towards him. Her eyes were full of alarm.

'How touching.'

Bergerac swung round as the nun emerged from behind the door. Norma Jean Veldman herself. Marilyn to her friends. In her hand was an automatic, a Beretta Modello 1934 with a long silencer. Bergerac stood up slowly, trying to shield Susan. A part of his mind was still functioning lucidly. It chose to remind him that the Beretta had a seven-round box magazine. Seven chances of death.

'The gallant sergeant,' Veldman said. 'It's no use, you know. You're in no state to do anything.'

Bergerac took a step towards her.

She sighed. 'Another inch closer, and I start shooting. I've nothing left to lose, so don't try that argument.'

'Give me the gun,' Bergerac said hoarsely.

'Don't be stupid, Bergerac. You've run out of options. You're going to help me. If you won't cooperate, then you'll all have to die.' She smiled and pointed with the gun. 'First you. Then that silly little girl of yours. And then, last of all, my father.'

CHAPTER
18

Veldman's finger tightened on the trigger of the automatic.

Bergerac swayed forwards. Susan tensed her muscles, though she knew she was incapable of intervening. Veldman permitted herself a little smile.

'Go on, Sergeant,' she cooed. 'It really would be a pleasure.'

The smile froze. Bergerac wasn't swaying: he was falling. Veldman slashed downwards with the barrel of the gun; the blow connected with Bergerac's head and deflected his fall by a few degrees. Susan made a wordless sound of protest. He sprawled face down on the floor.

Veldman knelt beside him, the black skirts of her habit billowing gracefully around her. She glanced at Susan.

'Don't worry, dear,' she said sweetly; it was the sort of sweetness that sets your teeth on edge. 'I think he's only fainted. Probably the safest thing he could do, in the circumstances.' She looked at her watch and stood up. 'As I was saying before we were so rudely interrupted: I'm going to untie you. It's time we left.'

She laid the gun on the bed and unknotted the gag.

Susan spat out the wadded handkerchief in her mouth. She would have done anything for a drink of water.

'What are you going to do with us?' she whispered.

'All I ever wanted was a little privacy with my father,' Veldman said. 'You're going to help me get it.' She squatted on her haunches and undid Susan's legs. 'The trouble is, this nasty little bungalow seems to be turning into Piccadilly Circus, thanks to you and the sergeant. It's only fair you should help me solve the problem you've created.' She moved up to the arms. 'We're going to your home, dear. You're an estate agent, so I'm sure it's somewhere nice and private. In any case, it'll have to do for the time being. I've run out of other options. Now, stand up slowly, and don't try anything stupid.'

Susan obeyed. Her wrists and ankles were badly chafed, but otherwise she was all right; she had been tied up only for half an hour.

Veldman backed away. She had the gun in her hand again.

'We'll use your jeep – it'll look less conspicuous outside your house. You'll do the driving, but don't let that give you any ideas. I've checked your driving licence and the map, so I know exactly where we're going and how we're getting there.'

'It won't work,' Susan said. 'A friend might come round, or – '

'Then you'll just have to find a reason to send them away again.' The blue eyes sparkled. 'Or else lover-boy will get a bullet in his head. Or possibly somewhere else that's less immediately fatal but far more painful.'

There was a slim chance, Susan realized, that delaying tactics could save their lives. Hobson knew she was here. Bergerac should have told the Bureau where he was going, though at present nothing about his actions could be taken for granted. Even now, a police car might be on its way to Maufant.

'And just how are you going to get off the island?' Susan asked. She was terrified, and she found a temporary refuge in anger. Her voice rose: 'You know something? You're mad.'

'No, just desperate.' The woman sounded unruffled but her eyes flickered round the room – from Bergerac to her father, and then back to Susan. 'I haven't exactly got much to lose, have I, dear?'

The repeated use of that meaningless endearment made Susan want to scream. But she recognized that Veldman had a point: British justice had already done its worst to her. She was a convicted multi-murderer, unlikely to get parole. They couldn't hang her for another killing or two: they could merely send her back to jail.

'You'll have to carry my father,' Veldman went on. 'He's dead to the world.'

Susan looked at the man in the cupboard. Just before Bergerac's arrival, Veldman had made her untie Robert Wetherby and remove the gag. His eyes were still closed. He was breathing, slowly and noisily. The blood on his face had dried. It came from two shallow cuts on his cheeks.

'The softening-up process,' Veldman murmured to herself. 'And now I shall have to start all over again.' She shivered unexpectedly and looked away. 'Once he's in the jeep, we'll come back for your copper.'

'I can't carry Jim,' Susan said. 'He's much too heavy for me.'

'I wish you'd stop making these silly little objections. You'll manage to move him somehow. Otherwise I'll just have to kill him here and now.' Veldman pulled the jeep's keys from her pocket and jingled them.

Her back to Veldman, Susan bent down and gave Wetherby a gentle shake. He groaned softly.

'Just get him under the armpits and haul him up,' Veldman snapped. 'Quickly, you stupid cow.'

Wetherby was no heavier than Susan. Age had pared away any surplus flesh he might once have had. As she pulled him upwards, his head lolled forward. *Dead to the world.* His chin, white with two days' worth of stubble, scraped against the thin silk of her shirt. As the head reached the level of her shoulder, it fell backwards. Susan glanced down at the face and almost screamed.

The eyes were open. Not just that, they were alert.

Immediately the lids fluttered down again. The head was

173

still back, as though Wetherby were unconscious; but Susan could feel him gradually taking his own weight.

'Pull him into the hall,' Veldman ordered. 'And remember, dear – I'm right beside you.'

Susan dragged the inert body across the carpet. Veldman was standing near the doorway, just inside the room. The gun was levelled at Susan.

As they passed through the doorway, Susan was no longer in the direct line of fire: Wetherby was between her and the Beretta. The old man chose that moment to make his move. He raised his arms, slipped out of her grip and turned round.

The second that followed was a foretaste of eternity. Susan, still facing into the room, would have liked time to have stopped altogether; the future was too terrifying to envisage. Veldman's face, incongruously framed by the wimple she wore over her head, showed a curious blend of anticipation and fear.

Why is she afraid?

'*Run*, Susan,' Wetherby said, without turning.

Automatically, Susan backed towards the front door.

Veldman raised the gun in both hands. The muzzle was pointing at Wetherby's head.

'No,' Susan gasped. 'No, please – '

Neither Wetherby nor his daughter seemed aware of her presence for all the notice they took of her. They were locked in a private struggle.

'Don't tempt me,' Veldman said harshly. 'I've waited long enough.'

'You won't shoot me,' the old man said. His voice was unsteady, but not with fear. 'You'll never be quite brave enough for that. Besides, you need me. Don't you, Jean?'

Jean?

'Need you?' Veldman screamed. 'I've never needed you.'

Susan's hand found the door-handle. Still watching the doorway where Wetherby stood, she pushed it down and tugged. Nothing happened. The front door was locked. And Veldman had the key.

'Without me,' Wetherby went on as if his daughter hadn't spoken, 'you wouldn't have a purpose in life.' His voice was hoarse but gathering strength. 'It would mean precisely *nothing*.'

'You think I do everything just to shock you?' she demanded. 'You really think that?'

'Yes. And I am terribly afraid I am right.'

Veldman moved a foot closer. She took a deep breath and steadied the pistol.

Suddenly Susan's paralysis loosed its grip on her. She made a dash for the door of the sitting room. The window was open. The curtains swayed in the breeze. Out there lay safety. Freedom was within reach. Freedom meant anywhere that didn't contain that big, blue-eyed woman.

But was freedom without Jim worth having?

'No,' Wetherby said sadly. 'This is one sin you do not have the courage to commit.'

Despite herself, Susan turned back.

The old clergyman was still blocking the doorway. He was leaning against the jamb. His head was bowed. The gun was steady in his daughter's hands.

'Make a rush for me,' Veldman said angrily. 'Go on. Show some guts for once in your life.'

Wetherby shook his head.

'Then stop smiling, you old bastard!'

Veldman's face was dead white; her mouth was open and her eyes stared at her father. He raised his head, as if staring back.

The gun barrel shook. Veldman blinked and slowly lowered the pistol. Through the crack between the jamb and Wetherby's body, Susan watched it descending, inch by inch.

When it reached the level of Veldman's hip there was a sudden flurry of movement.

A hand appeared, seemingly from nowhere, and wrapped itself round Veldman's wrist. Veldman toppled sideways. Susan ran forwards, pushing past Wetherby. The old man's lips were moving, as if he was praying silently.

Bergerac was still holding the wrist of Veldman's gun hand, pressing it into the carpet; but she was on top of him and struggling violently. As Susan plunged through the doorway, Bergerac shouted in agony.

She acted instinctively: she stamped with all her might on the hand that held the Beretta. Veldman's fingers relaxed their hold. Susan kicked the gun away. The thin leather of her shoe gave little protection, and her toe exploded with pain. The pistol rose clear of the carpet, sailed through the doorway and crashed on to the parquet floor of the hall. It skidded a yard and came to rest by the sitting-room door.

Veldman rolled away from Bergerac and, impeded by her clothes, clambered to her feet. The clasp-knife and the keys of the jeep fell from one of her pockets. Susan tried to stop her from reaching the door. Veldman punched her on the nose, sending her reeling back against the bed.

Wetherby had moved from the doorway and was trying ineffectually to help Bergerac up.

They were too late. Veldman burst into the hall and flung herself bodily on to the gun.

Wetherby let go of Bergerac's arm. With a decisiveness that contrasted sharply with his previous movements, he swung round and slammed the door. The key was on the inside. He turned it in the lock.

'Get away from the door,' Bergerac croaked. 'Against the wall.'

Wetherby obeyed. Susan was already away from any possible line of fire. Bergerac crawled over to her. She touched his hand. He grimaced at her in what might have been an attempt to smile.

'Open the door,' Veldman said. 'Or I'll shoot the lock off.'

Bergerac raised his voice. 'They only do that in the movies. It's harder than it looks, especially with the Beretta's calibre. And of course the ricochets won't be very healthy for you.'

'I'll count to five,' Veldman shouted. 'One – '

'The police will be here at any moment. Use your head, Norma Jean. Call it a day.'

'The window?' Susan whispered urgently.

'We'll face that if it comes. Hush.'

Bergerac slithered on his stomach across the floor. He scooped up the knife and edged back to the shelter of the bed.

There was silence on the other side of the door. The blood was running down Susan's face and dripping on the carpet. She tried to staunch the flow with her sleeve and glanced at Wetherby. His lips were moving again. Maybe there was something to be said for the power of prayer, after all.

The silence stretched from seconds to minutes.

'What's happening, for God's sake?' Susan said. 'Is she trying the sitting-room window? We'd have heard the front door.'

Somewhere outside, a starter motor whirred and an engine fired.

Bergerac hauled himself up. 'Hear that?' His voice was strong with outrage. 'She's gone and nicked my car.'

'I don't know about you,' Charlie Hungerford said, 'but I could do with a drink.' He opened the cabinet and took out two glasses. 'Scotch OK for you?'

'Fine,' Prinknash said. 'Just a dash of water and no ice, please.'

The neck of the bottle rattled against the glass.

'Beats me how you can be so calm, Vernon. That woman's lethal.'

'There's nothing to worry about.' Prinknash, who was ensconced in one of the deep leather armchairs with a copy of *Sea Angler* on his lap, suppressed a yawn. 'They've got men on the gate, in the grounds and in the house. They're combing the island for her. She hasn't got a chance. In a way, I feel almost sorry for her.'

'*Sorry* for her!' Whisky slopped from the glass in Hungerford's hand and splashed on the cabinet. 'You can't mean that.'

'But I do. And the whole world is going to know. I made that quite clear in the interview.'

Just after their arrival at the house, the BBC had called. Prinknash had been interviewed over the telephone.

'It'll be on the national news,' he went on with barely concealed satisfaction. 'The point I was trying to make is that one has to stand up to this sort of personal terrorism. One can't afford to show fear.' He paused, smiling. 'I mentioned you, actually. I hope you don't mind.'

Hungerford handed the whisky to Prinknash. 'Really? Er – what did you say?'

'I said the friend I was staying with quite agreed with me on the need to take a strong stand – had pressed me to stay, despite the danger – refused to bow to pressure – you know the sort of thing.'

'Did – ah – did you happen to mention my name?'

'Of course. Charles Hungerford, I said, the well-known Jersey millionaire and Chairman of the Law and Order Committee.' Prinknash sipped his whisky. 'It's a small return for all your hospitality. I imagine a little publicity won't do you any harm.'

'That's very civil of you, Vernon. I appreciate it.'

Hungerford glanced at the clock: fifteen minutes to go to the next news bulletin. He would have to record the broadcast for his video library. It would be some compensation for all the worry. He sat down and took a long swallow of his drink.

'But . . .' He took another swallow. 'Supposing she *does* get through the guards?'

Prinknash shrugged. 'Naturally I've considered the possibility, remote though it is. We'll cope. Look.'

He opened his double-breasted jacket.

Hungerford's mouth fell open. 'Do you always carry that around with you?'

'Only when it might be useful. It's perfectly legal, by the way – I've got a licence. So there's nothing to worry about, is there?'

'Come on,' Bergerac said. 'We've got to get after her.'

'Leave it, Jim,' Susan pleaded. 'Let someone else take over.'

'There's no time, love – she's armed.'

'Well, you'll let me drive. You're in no state to –'

But Bergerac wasn't listening. 'Ring the Bureau,' he said to Wetherby. 'They'll send a car for you.'

Susan picked up the keys, ready to hold on to them by force if Bergerac tried to take them away from her.

The old man shook his head. 'I'm coming with you.'

There was only one thing left to do – one hope of safety; one chance of freedom.

So far she had been damned unlucky. It was all because of her father. Everything was because of him. She should have killed him, back there. He had no right to be so – what was the word?

Invulnerable.

But maybe the tide had turned. Norma Jean Veldman was privately superstitious: the fact that Bergerac had left his car keys in the ignition seemed like a good omen.

She reversed away from the bungalow, grinding the unfamiliar gears, and roared into the narrow access road.

Halfway down she caught up with a tractor, which was going in the same direction. The driver refused to pull over to let her pass. *A bad omen?* She honked the horn; she rolled down the window and swore at him; but the old man ignored her. *The bloody obstinate peasant.* The precious seconds ticked away. It would be satisfying to shoot the old fool, but that would waste even more time in the end.

At the T-junction the tractor pulled over to the right. Veldman shot through on the inside. She turned left and accelerated away.

Suppose the hope failed? Suppose the chance was no chance at all? Suppose she was putting her head in a trap?

Well, in that case there would be only one thing left.

Vengeance.

DC Willy Pettit was in charge of the detail at the gate. He was having a wonderful time.

He was the temporary lord and master of two uniformed constables. For the first time in his career, he had been issued with a gun, a heavy, standard-issue revolver. He secretly wished it were possible for someone to take a photograph of him. As a souvenir.

The iron gates were closed and locked. They were an important part of the defences because there was no other way a car could get into Hungerford's grounds. A rumour was going the rounds to the effect that a TV team might be coming to the house. They would have to pass through the gates. More than likely they'd want a few outside shots.

Jeff Yardley touched Pettit's arm. 'I can hear a car.'

Pettit peered through the gates. The road, little more than a lane, curved away on either side; he could see nearly a hundred yards in each direction.

The Triumph Roadster rounded a corner at speed. Its horn blared.

'Open up,' Pettit said. 'It's Dauntless Jim, and he's in his usual hurry.'

While Yardley and his colleague obeyed the order, Pettit radioed up to the makeshift control room in Hungerford's dining room.

'Barry? Bergerac's on his way up to the house.'

The gates swung open on silent, well-oiled hinges.

Two seconds later, the Triumph was upon them. Barely slackening speed, it surged into the driveway, scraping one wing against a gate and forcing Pettit to leap aside. He slipped on the grassy verge and ended up on his back.

'The maniac – who does he think he is?'

Then Pettit glimpsed the driver's face. For a split second, a vision of his future career in the States Police rose up before him. In ruins.

He fumbled for the radio. 'Barry! It's *Veldman!*'

Veldman braked, just in time.

The wheels locked, skidding on the gravel. The Triumph slid, rather than rolled, into the gap between Hungerford's Rolls and the grey Bristol Beaufighter. In front of her was the blank wall of the house. For the moment, she had cover on three sides. At present she needed all the help she could get. She had expected a token police guard on the house, not the small army that seemed to be in residence.

She scrambled out and crouched by Prinknash's car. Three men were coming up the drive; two others were zigzagging across the lawn. The front door opened, attracting her attention to a threat that was closer to hand.

'Put down your weapon. Come out slowly with your hands on your head.'

Veldman peered round the back of the car. A slim plain-clothes man was standing in the doorway, partly sheltered by the heavy front door. She fired once.

The shot missed, as she had suspected it would; but nevertheless it achieved the effect she wanted. The man ducked back into the house.

It was now or never. Six shots left; the spare magazines

were still at the bungalow. Veldman left the cars and sprinted for the corner of the house, away from the men on the drive and the lawn. A low wall loomed ahead. She scrambled over it and found herself on a stone-flagged terrace; a series of french windows linked it with the house.

Another party of men was approaching the house from this side of the garden; but unless they had rifles, they didn't have a chance of stopping her.

She tried the nearest window. It was locked. Someone was moving in the room. She fired through the glass – *five shots left* – and opened the window from the inside.

Sir Vernon Prinknash was sitting in an armchair, smiling at her.

Charlie Hungerford was on his feet, backing towards the door with his hands held out as though he hoped they would ward off a bullet.

'Stop,' Veldman said. She moved aside from the window and got her back against the wall. 'Right. Lock the door. *Move!*'

Hungerford obeyed her. As he turned the key, he looked over his shoulder. 'My dear young lady, I'm sure we can – '

'Shut up. If you cooperate, you live. Got that?'

Hungerford nodded. Prinknash said nothing. He was still smiling. Veldman looked at him, waiting for an answer.

There were footsteps on the terrace. Then silence. Then the sound of a car coming up the drive. Veldman could imagine the whispered orders and the marksmen running for position. The police would use the standard procedure for sieges involving hostages. But it wouldn't work, because this wasn't a standard siege. There was a joker in this pack, and she had him in her hand.

'Stop him!' someone hissed outside.

Veldman spun round. A man was standing by the open french window, looking into the room.

Her father. *Daddy . . .*

'I want to talk to you, Jean,' he said gently. 'I'm coming in.'

It all happened so quickly. First, something snapped in her head. She felt both sad and relieved. For once in her life she was free. No more prisons, no more rules, no more doubts and no more needs: free. *So why can't I be happy, too?* She left the question unanswered and raised the gun. It was the only answer she had left.

Then, as she pulled the trigger, there was a blur of movement on the terrace. She heard someone shouting.

That bastard Bergerac –

And then, finally, there was nothing at all.

The Reverend Robert Wetherby knelt beside his daughter's body. His lips were moving silently. His face was calm, even stern.

Norma Jean Veldman lay across the lintel of the french windows. The bullet had followed a rising trajectory through the back of her skull and blown away the top of her head.

Bergerac, supported by Goddard, squeezed past Wetherby. His left hand was clamped over his right forearm. Blood oozed through fingers. The bullet from the Beretta had punched a clean hole through the flesh. Susan, biting her lip, followed the two policemen into the room.

Hungerford hurried forward, averting his eyes from the mess on the terrace.

'Well, thank God for that,' he said hoarsely. 'She'd have killed us if Vernon hadn't . . .'

Bergerac pulled himself away from Goddard and pushed past Hungerford. Prinknash was still sitting in the armchair. He was no longer smiling. The Walther PPK was now resting on the arm of the chair.

'I had no choice, Jim,' Prinknash said.

'Aye, that's right,' Hungerford agreed. 'Justifiable manslaughter. Saved your life, I shouldn't wonder.'

'Manslaughter?' Bergerac's face was covered with blotches of angry skin. He picked up the Walther. 'Sir Vernon Prinknash,' he said formally, 'I am arresting you on a charge of murder. I must warn you – '

Bergerac's legs gave way. He collapsed in a huddle against the chair.

There was a moment's silence.

Then Susan ran forward and knelt beside him.

'Well, *do* something,' she snapped, without looking up.

She eased him into a more comfortable position and loosened the collar of his shirt. Beneath the shirt, the skin was flushed; and the flush was speckled with tiny red spots. She fought back a hysterical desire to laugh.

'Is Jim all right?' Hungerford asked. 'Just a flesh wound, eh?'

'No, it isn't just a flesh wound,' Susan said angrily. 'Can't you see he's got scarlet fever?'

CHAPTER
19

It was not until the following Thursday that Bergerac was allowed visitors.

The week in bed had gone a long way towards healing his body, but it had also left his mind starved of news. The doctor had ordered him to avoid excitement. Susan had taken time off work to make sure that Bergerac obeyed. In consequence, he was thoroughly bored, and his head was full of questions in search of answers.

On the Thursday, however, he took part in three separate conversations, all of which were important. Some of the questions were answered. Others he didn't even ask. And some, of course, were unanswerable.

The first caller, Barney Crozier, came in the morning.

'Don't tire him,' Susan said as she left the room.

'How long are you going to be off-duty?' Crozier demanded. 'You just wouldn't believe the paperwork this case requires.'

'The doctor says at least another week,' Bergerac said. He was sitting in an armchair by the window. 'Assuming I don't get rheumatic fever or acute nephritis.'

'You're having me on?'

Bergerac shook his head. 'They're possible complications of scarlet fever. Possible but unlikely.'

'Well, you can't afford to have them, Sergeant. Is that clear?'

'Yes, sir,' Bergerac said solemnly, trying to conceal his relief.

Neither of them mentioned Bergerac's unauthorized trip to France while on sick leave; neither of them brought up the disciplinary action that Crozier had threatened. If Crozier chose to forget, who was Bergerac to remind him?

'The Prinknash case,' Crozier said abruptly. 'Want to hear about it?'

Bergerac nodded. 'Is he talking?'

'Prinknash isn't the chatty type, unfortunately. But we've pieced together most of it. As Wilson told you, he was Scowles' executor. He's also on the verge of bankruptcy – the usual story: overextended his investments and lost a packet in the crash last year. He knew that Veldman was Wetherby's daughter because of something that Scowles had let slip. So Prinknash contacted Veldman and made a deal: her freedom and fifty per cent of the money; in return, she'd do the work and let him have the rest. He put up the money to have her sprung out of jail. She found the people to do it. The idea was that they'd snatch Wetherby and force him to sign a deed of gift in favour of a fake charity. Prinknash did the paperwork. He set up a dummy firm, Apley and Tuke, with a one-room office and no employees, ostensibly to run the charity's financial affairs. And Apley and Tuke itself was just a front for a whole series of off-the-peg Liberian companies, registered in Liechtenstein. We think that eventually the money was to be siphoned into an Austrian bank account and divided. Very neat – it'll take us months to work it all out.'

'It would have worked,' Bergerac said slowly, 'if it hadn't been for Wetherby.'

'He must be tough as old boots,' Crozier said. 'I don't pretend to understand him.'

Susan stuck her head in the room. 'You won't be long, will you, Barney?'

'Just another minute,' he said absently.

'You've connected Prinknash with Stroat?' Bergerac said.

'All Stroat wanted was a little dirt on Prinknash's sex-life. Instead he overheard the meeting with Thornber at the Orchid Factory: Prinknash needed to know about the changed arrangements for Veldman's arrival on Jersey. Stroat didn't realize what he was getting into. He went along to St Vimy's Bay to see what the tide brought in. And Veldman saw him. She terrorized Thornber into silence. He was out of his depth, too.'

'Prinknash knew she'd killed Stroat?'

Crozier grunted. 'Of course he did. He's no fool. It didn't worry him particularly, as far as I can tell, any more than it did Veldman.'

'Two of a kind,' Bergerac said. 'Under the skin.'

'Maybe. Could be that Prinknash killed too many people in Korea.' Crozier shrugged: he was unhappy with speculation at the best of times. 'Veldman tried to kill you when she found out you'd seen Thornber. And she killed Thornber because he was becoming a liability. It makes me sweat to think she'd probably have got away with it if Susan hadn't seen Prinknash's car outside the bungalow.'

Bergerac laughed. 'You've got to hand it to him – Prinknash, I mean. I presume he invented the whole business about a death threat?'

'I imagine it was just to get a little free publicity for his political career. And perhaps to help cover himself if Veldman was caught.'

'She must have gone to him for help. The last resort.'

'Or to kill him. She had nothing left. After all, it was his idea. And it had failed.'

'Her father upset her,' Bergerac said. 'It was like they had a battle of wills, and he won. That somehow he always won.'

Crozier frowned. 'I leave that sort of thing to the psychiatrists,' he said. 'Nothing to do with us.'

'That's enough, Barney.' Susan was standing in the doorway with her hands on her hips. 'I'm not having him talking about work and tiring himself out. You can come back tomorrow if you want.'

'Sue . . .' Bergerac said.

Crozier stood up. 'Yes, Susan,' he said meekly.

After the invalid had finished his lunch and had his rest, Wetherby tiptoed into the bedroom behind Susan.

'Robert,' Bergerac said. 'I'm glad you came.'

'Are you sure you're well enough?' Wetherby asked anxiously. 'I could always come back another day.'

'I'm much better,' Bergerac said quickly, with a glance at Susan. 'The rash has gone, the temperature's down, my throat feels fine. And I'm not infectious. The rest of me's back to normal, more or less. To tell you the truth, I'm bored. You're doing me a favour by coming.'

The old man sat down slowly on the chair beside the bed. Susan said, 'I'll make some tea,' to no one in particular, and left the room.

'I didn't keep away because of the scarlet fever,' Wetherby said.

'I know. I'm . . . I'm sorry about your daughter.'

Wetherby nodded. 'She was always my daughter,' he said quietly. 'I blame myself, you know.'

'Why?'

'Jean's mother died when she was a toddler. I was a bad father – she needed someone young who had plenty of time for her. I was tied up with my work and too set in my ways. I didn't give her enough of myself, I'm afraid.'

'You don't have to tell me this,' Bergerac said.

'It's better that you know,' Wetherby said. 'I would like you to understand.'

'All right. If you're sure.'

'She was a violent child. It was a tough, East End parish, and she found plenty of temptations. She got away from me as soon as she could. Then she met Veldman and started calling herself *Norma* Jean . . . He was a drug addict; the marriage didn't last. Sometimes she sent me cuttings from newspapers. No message – just a few inches of newsprint about some crime or another. That's when I started drinking seriously.'

'It's over now,' Bergerac said.

'You think so?' Wetherby smiled wryly. 'The psychiatrists had a label for her but that's all it was: just a label, not an answer or an explanation. Now she's dead, it doesn't mean I can stop trying to find out *why*.'

In the silence that followed he pulled a large envelope from his pocket and laid it on the bedside table.

'That's for you, Jim.'

Bergerac opened the envelope. Inside was a travelling chess-set, in a carved walnut box. The delicately carved pieces, Bergerac remembered, were made of ivory and ebony; and the inlaid squares of the board were ebony and sandalwood. It was Kashmiri work, at least fifty years old. Wetherby did not have many possessions; and this was one of the few that had any intrinsic value.

'You can't give me this,' Bergerac said, flushing. 'I won't accept it.'

Wetherby stood up. 'I want you to have it,' he said simply. 'May I come and see you again tomorrow? Perhaps we could have a game.'

Bergerac nodded. Suddenly he felt very tired. 'You owe me a victory.'

The last conversation was with Susan.

Wetherby had left but the pot of tea needed to be drunk. She sat on the bed with him.

'Sue?'

'What?'

'Thanks.'

There was a silence.

'Sue?'

'What?'

'Let's go away. Catch a plane. Go somewhere hot for a week. Pretend this business didn't happen ... Pretend we've just met, and it's all beginning.'

'All right.' She turned away to straighten the covers so that he couldn't see her face. Suddenly she looked directly at him. 'If you're sure you want to.'

'I'm sure,' Bergerac said.

Susan said, 'I wonder,' and then she bent and kissed him unromantically on the nose.

FOR THE BEST IN PAPERBACKS, LOOK FOR THE

In every corner of the world, on every subject under the sun, Penguin represents quality and variety – the very best in publishing today.

For complete information about books available from Penguin – including Pelicans, Puffins, Peregrines and Penguin Classics – and how to order them, write to us at the appropriate address below. Please note that for copyright reasons the selection of books varies from country to country.

In the United Kingdom: For a complete list of books available from Penguin in the U.K., please write to *Dept E.P., Penguin Books Ltd, Harmondsworth, Middlesex, UB7 0DA*

In the United States: For a complete list of books available from Penguin in the U.S., please write to *Dept BA, Penguin, 299 Murray Hill Parkway, East Rutherford, New Jersey 07073*

In Canada: For a complete list of books available from Penguin in Canada, please write to *Penguin Books Canada Ltd, 2801 John Street, Markham, Ontario L3R 1B4*

In Australia: For a complete list of books available from Penguin in Australia, please write to the *Marketing Department, Penguin Books Australia Ltd, P.O. Box 257, Ringwood, Victoria 3134*

In New Zealand: For a complete list of books available from Penguin in New Zealand, please write to the *Marketing Department, Penguin Books (NZ) Ltd, Private Bag, Takapuna, Auckland 9*

In India: For a complete list of books available from Penguin, please write to *Penguin Overseas Ltd, 706 Eros Apartments, 56 Nehru Place, New Delhi, 110019*

In Holland: For a complete list of books available from Penguin in Holland, please write to *Penguin Books Nederland B.V., Postbus 195, NL–1380AD Weesp, Netherlands*

In Germany: For a complete list of books available from Penguin, please write to *Penguin Books Ltd, Friedrichstrasse 10 – 12, D–6000 Frankfurt Main 1, Federal Republic of Germany*

In Spain: For a complete list of books available from Penguin in Spain, please write to *Longman Penguin España, Calle San Nicolas 15, E–28013 Madrid, Spain*